Demon Cursed

by

Karilyn Bentley

A Demon Huntress Novel

Demon Cursed

Cover Art by *Diana Carlile*

The Wild Rose Press, Inc.
PO Box 708
Adams Basin, NY 14410-0708
Visit us at www.thewildrosepress.com

Publishing History
First Mainstream Paranormal Edition, 2017
Print ISBN 978-1-5092-1342-9
Digital ISBN 978-1-5092-1343-6

A Demon Huntress Novel
Published in the United States of America

I shake my head at him

before straightening my shoulders. And slapping a hand over my mouth and nose. Yuck. Hours-old death in humid Texas weather makes for a smelly situation. At least I'm not the only one with their hand, or handkerchief, over their mouths.

"What happened?" Smythe meets the gaze of each guard and the hyperventilating janitorial women who clearly found the body.

One of the women points to where the body lies in front of the Dumpster, flat on her back, hands resting in classic death pose on her bloody stabbed chest, a red rose clasped in her fingers. Her open eyes stare into the night, her mouth curled into a grimace of pain and death. Her clothes look like she came from a club: tight, short, and low-cut, with spiky heels. At one time, I would've been jealous of her hot-to-trot figure.

Now all I notice is the pain and terror stamped on her face and the unfurling anger deep in my core. Fucking murderers. I might be a fancy-assed demon huntress, but I destroy minions, not human killers. Lucky for me, I can tell which type of kill this scene belongs to with little effort.

Closing my eyes, I start to take a deep calming breath, think better of it, and focus on activating my minion sensors. Tapping into the power of the entity lying along my nerves, I open my eyes to a tactical grid display of reds and oranges, a clear indication of a minion's presence at the scene.

Looks like I'll get my wish to annihilate the fucking bastard who killed this poor woman.

Dedications

To the best beta readers ever,
J.C. McKenzie and Carrie Hamlin.
You help me out in more ways than I can say.
~*~
And to my wonderful hubby.
Without your encouragement,
these books would not exist. I love you!

Chapter One

My stomach slams into a metal railing as surgically enhanced double D's press into my back. Cheap beer soaks my arm. A not-so-feminine yell shatters my eardrums. For a second, a similar incident during my whiskey-fueled college years flitters in my mind. I shove the memory back into hiding, and return to the present. Quick reflexes stop me from tumbling over the railing to land on the pissed-off crowd below our box seats. Jackie lets loose a string of obscenities directed at the ref on the field below us, but at least she moves her body off mine.

Thank God. Death by double D's at a football game is not the way I thought I'd go.

The crowd goes wild as I suck back air, trying to recover from my near-death experience. Jackie, my twin brother T's blonde bimbo girlfriend, along with everyone else, screams at the ref's call. Only a ref would call a catch that phenomenal in the last five seconds of the game a missed pass. A call which caused our NFL team, the Arlington Armadillos, to lose.

Which in turn causes a crowd of beer-drenched, adrenaline-pumped humans to scream in anguish.

"Here, Gin." T hands me a beer as I straighten, rubbing my stomach. Good thing I wear a *justitia*, a demon-fighting bracelet that gives me quick healing powers. By the time I finish the beer, the pain and bruising in my stomach will be gone.

I take a swallow of cheap beer. If only the tickets T won off the radio included better beer instead of the watery version filling my cup. Not that I'm complaining. Beer is beer, after all.

"Is the ref smoking dope?" T asks, sloshing beer over the rim of his cup as he uses it to point at the field.

"Sure seems that way." Clearly the refs were in cahoots to prevent us from winning.

The woes of being a die-hard football fan: seeing conspiracy theories at every call.

I glance over my shoulder, into the suite, where mage Aidan Smythe sits on a sofa, his feet propped on the coffee table, surrounded by empty beer bottles and cups. Smythe's fingers fly across the keyboard of his laptop. Only my mentor would show up to a football game and perform Internet searches for demon activity instead of watching the game.

Mages. Impossible to understand. Impossible to slap out their crazy.

"Hey, babe…" Jackie sashays to T, boobs first. "When do we get to meet the team?"

"It's not the whole team. Only a couple of them. And the DJs are supposed to get us."

With a lucky call, T won game tickets from the local radio station during a contest for a Thursday night home game. Access to a private suite, all the beer we can drink, and a buffet were included in the package. A photo op with the morning show DJs occurred prior to the game. The highlight of the evening was coming after the game: meet-n-greet passes for some of the team.

We hadn't been told which team members were

participating. Jackie wanted to meet Donald Merryweather, aka Donny Football, the wide receiver known for his face time in the media for everything from children's charities to animal rescue. Organizations lined up to use him as their spokesperson.

What a nice guy. Someone not afraid to give away money to special causes—even if he required media exposure to be generous.

So what if he wanted people to know he's the face of certain charities instead of donating anonymously? As long as he catches the ball and scores touchdowns, who cares?

"Guess I need to tell Smythe to put away his laptop before the DJs arrive."

T shakes his head at my mentor. When I first slipped on my demon-killing bracelet—the *justitia*—I was assigned a guardian mage, my mentor Smythe, whose main job seems to be saving my ass.

Not that my ass has needed saving lately, but when I first started this gig I almost died. *A lot.* Smythe always swooped in to save the day, ahem, I mean my life. A girl can do with a little life-saving action. Especially when the life saver is six foot five inches of black-haired, blue-eyed eye candy. Yep, he's pleasing to look at, but so are plenty of other men.

None of whom cook for me, save my life, or listen to me grouch. None but Aidan Smythe, mentor extraordinaire.

His only fault being an unhealthy attachment to his laptop.

"Man…" T gestures at Smythe with his beer. Smythe glances up from the interesting info flying across his screen. "Who the hell plays around on their computer instead of watching the game?"

"Not my team." Smythe shrugs.

"Who the hell lives in Dallas and doesn't cheer for the Armadillos?"

"I don't live in Dallas. I'm on permanent loan here."

"Po-tay-toe, po-tah-toe." I wave a hand. Offer him a grin. His eyes twinkle, and my middle sinks into an unwanted puddle of desire.

I clearly have problems. Bosses, including mentors, are off limits for a reason. Namely potential workplace problems if the relationship ends. At least that's what I've been telling myself. But over the last three months of working together, the reason grows fuzzy, and tries to rationalize itself right between the sheets for some horizontal action.

I lock down my thoughts, build barriers around them, as Smythe's lips turn into a grin. As if he reads my mind. He shouldn't be able to do that anymore unless I project my thoughts. He's taught me well.

And yet I get the distinct impression he sees right into my mind and reads my inner desires, secrets, and lies.

I shudder. Nope. Not going there. Not thinking it. *Am. Not. Thinking. It.*

"So, how much longer—" A knock interrupts my sentence.

Saved by the arriving DJs.

T opens the suite door, ushering in Crazy Larry, who lives up to his name, and Little India, who is neither little nor Indian. Instead of a petite Indian woman, Little India stands over six feet tall with bone-china-white skin, black hair, and enough piercings to set off a metal detector from fifty yards away.

"Hey, hey, hey." Crazy Larry slaps T on the shoulder. "Sorry the game was a bummer." Two steps later and he fills up a cup with the beer on tap. We all watch as he swallows it down in one gulp like he's a college frat boy instead of a sixty-something gray-haired skinny little fella.

Can you say refusal to grow up?

I plaster a smile on my face as he does a shimmy, whooping and hollering like the crazy DJ he is. Seeing him gives me even more incentive to stay on the straight and narrow. I set my beer on the counter.

"Well, now that the game's over, let's go meet the team!" Crazy Larry pours himself another beer and starts for the door.

"Will Donny Football be there?" Jackie grabs T's arm, eyes wide with anticipation.

T glares as if he's shocked she finds someone besides him attractive. Not sure why he's surprised, I know for a fact he finds other women attractive. Mainly one woman. Eloise. A healer for the Agency, my employer for the new demon-killing gig. Eloise rocks.

Unfortunately, large boobs and a ditzy smile sway T more than brains and the ability to heal injuries.

Stay out of my head. T turns his glare to me.

It doesn't take a telepathic twin to know how you feel about Eloise.

One of the perks of being twins is using telepathy to talk to each other. Not sure if other twins can do this, I never bothered to ask.

T wraps an arm around Jackie's waist, yanks her closer, and plants a kiss on her cheek. As if to give me the middle finger.

Brothers.

Little India answers Jackie since her radio partner walked out the door as if he didn't hear the question. "We're not sure which players will be there. I hope Donny will. He's hot." She winks, her lids getting a workout from the excessive mascara coating her lashes.

Little India waggles her fingers as she follows her partner out the door. A click of a laptop closing followed by the squeak of couch springs tells me Smythe follows. I let T and Jackie go before me as I wait for my mentor. He puts his hand on the back of my neck, steering me out the door.

His skin-on-skin touch elicits no insight into his emotions, unlike the readings I get from every other person on the planet. Being an empath while trying to maintain a relationship never works out well.

Well, almost never. It worked with Blake. Until he was murdered by a demon.

Nope, not going there. Three months after my on-again off-again lover and full-time friend died and I'm almost adjusted to not having him around. Thinking about him makes things worse.

I focus on T and Jackie instead.

As if he reads my thoughts, which he can't due to my hard-as-steel mental barrier, Smythe drops his hand. The imprint of his touch leaves a warm spot on my skin that sinks into my core like…

Gah! Am I actually going to make some sort of lovesick comparison between a romance novel and us? I need to get laid as a way to erase a bad case of stupid hormones, but my empath ability makes that a little difficult. Okay, a lot difficult. Unless I'm high or buzzed. Which I no longer do. Usually. Go me.

Being on the straight and narrow has never been so hard.

"I'm so excited. This is going to be so much fun!" Jackie slurs, hanging on to T like he's a support beam.

Smythe sighs. I pat his shoulder. One side of his lips turns up. Solidarity in the face of ditziness.

We walk to the elevator, which takes us to ground level. When the doors open, we are directed down a long, concrete-walled hall into what I can only describe as a press room. Or a party suite.

Crazy Larry heads toward the bar and pours himself another beer while Little India presses her lips together and shoots him the stink eye. All is not well in the land of radio.

"Where are they?" Jackie looks around the room crowded with other back-stage pass holders, over-stuffed couches, plush chairs, and a bar with enough booze to keep a professional drunk happy for weeks. Liquor abounds, but the promised players are missing.

"They'll be here. Don't you worry your pretty little head none." Crazy Larry hands her a fresh beer while ignoring T's overprotective boyfriend glare.

But I really can't blame T. Jackie might be a couple of sandwiches short of a picnic, but hearing some skinny middle-aged guy patronize her with the "pretty little head" comment rankles.

Lost in his own beer, Crazy Larry remains clueless to the stares and glares. Before the tension ramps up another notch, the door crashes open, and a wall of security guards, followed by ten of the most popular team members, along with a handful of others I don't recognize, flow into the room.

Noise dominates, turning the quiet, tension-filled room into an after-party. Make that a pissed off after-party. No one likes to lose.

My *justitia* vibrates with a subtle hum, as if sensing a minion, the same buzz it gives when Smythe and I go to the Agency, a supposedly minion-free building. Confusion rattles the silver links, but at least it doesn't form a sword, its usual response to a minion. So what does it sense?

Over the last couple of months of being a *Justitian*—or as I like to refer to myself, a demon huntress—I've gotten used to knowing what my *justitia* thinks. The entity in the bracelet is fused to my nervous system and occasionally allows a glimpse into its memories of the *Justitians* who wore it before me. Usually when it senses a minion—a human playing host to a demon's essence—it forms a sword and I give the minion payback.

Which in this case typically ends in a loss of life for the minion.

But sometimes, like at the Agency and right now, my *justitia* senses what isn't there. I've yet to figure out why. Clearly there's a demon presence, minus the demon or minion. But where? Or who?

I should spend more time observing the players for demon influence, but hey, I'm a fan and would rather get their autographs and meet them than attempt my form of exorcism.

An excited squeal from Jackie snaps me out of my thoughts.

"Donny Football!"

Before I finish turning toward her, she's at the football star's side, giving him a hug. Not that he seems to mind her double D's pressing into his chest. T's right behind her, hand stuck out, arm wrapping around her waist as she releases Donny. The football star shakes T's hand and ignores my twin's she's-mine glare.

My opinion of Donny just went up a notch. His classic dark skin, black hair, and brown eyes might have helped. Along with a lean, muscular body.

He's like looking at art hanging on a museum's walls. Meant to admire from afar, not take home.

His gaze meets mine, and everything stills.

Okay, not really, but judging from how his gaze roams my body, he likes what he sees too.

Smythe steps beside me, extends his hand toward Donny, his jaw tense. As if he's mad. Or jealous.

I can dream. He probably just wants to get this meet-n-greet over with, so he can stare some more at his laptop screen.

Donny shakes Smythe's hand but keeps his gaze on me. Heat licks my cheeks.

"Hi. I'm Gin." Unlike the others, I clasp my hands together at my waist. I want to remain in fantasyland about how nice Donny is, not learn otherwise by an unwanted empath reading.

"Hi Gin. I'm Donny."

"I know." Way to fumble with words, Gin. I give a little finger wave in hope he fails to notice. "I mean, nice to meet you." Can my cheeks get any hotter? Geez.

He smiles. "The pleasure is all mine." The deep tenor of his voice rubs against my skin.

Tingles zip straight to my core, firing warmth in my lower belly. Yeah, I can see myself getting down and dirty with Donny, but why would I want to when Smythe stands by my side. I'd rather do the horizontal mamba with my mentor.

I'm not sure whether to be happy or sad with that realization.

I swallow. "Good game. Until that ref's call."

His lips press together. "I caught that damn ball."

"You did." Jackie touches his arm, and I can almost see the steam rise from T's head. "That ref was an idiot."

"A fucking idiot," T adds.

Smythe grips my shoulder. Still jealous? Yeah, right, whatever. I glance at him, but he's not even looking at us. His gaze fixates on the bar, on the crowd cheering on some drinker. Why does it not surprise me Crazy Larry stands on a chair, a beer in each hand, chugging one down?

I'm starting to get embarrassed for him.

Donny turns to the cheering crowd, his eyes narrowing. Crazy Larry notices and points an empty beer cup at Donny.

"It's Donny Slick-Fingered Football!" For a dude who's put away at least three beers in the last ten minutes, his words sound normal, not slurred.

And they hit their target.

The entire room falls silent, the only noise the pounding bass beat of the stereo. Donny seems to expand, as Crazy Larry's words strike sore nerves. The DJ seems oblivious to the impending session of whoop-ass heading his way. Little India tries to yank on his arm, but he shakes her off. After an eye roll and head shake, she turns her back on him and walks into the crowd. As if that was a cue, everyone but us and Donny starts talking again, ratcheting up the noise level.

Jackie reaches for Donny, but he's walking toward

Crazy Larry, the four of us following in his wake, as if to get a better view of the upcoming smackdown.

"That little punk is about to get his ass handed to him in a bag." Smythe shakes his head. "Stupid idiot."

"He probably thinks he's being funny."

Smythe shoots me a get-real glare. "Right, Gin. He has to know he's behaving like an ass."

My response freezes on my tongue as Donny steps up to Crazy Larry.

"What did you say?" Donny's hands ball at his sides, his voice vibrating with anger.

The DJ takes a sip of beer, playing like he doesn't see his death written in the football star's gaze. "I said, you were slick-fingered."

Donny's nostrils flare as leans toward Crazy Larry. "You sure you wanna go there with me?"

A security guard shoves me into Smythe, his touch so quick it barely leaves a read. The guard pulls Donny back several feet, stopping him from knocking Crazy Larry off the chair. Another guard grabs the DJ, ignoring his hey-hey-get-your-hands-off-me complaints.

Once again the room falls silent only to burst into noise as the main attraction gets pulled apart. Lesson learned: even charitable guys lose their temper when mocked by middle-aged drunk DJs.

Not that I blame Donny. Crazy Larry's escort out of the suite by security only brings cheers.

As soon as the DJ leaves, Donny relaxes, and the guard releases his arm. Just in time for a second guard to rush over to whisper in the first guard's ear. Donny ignores them both, opting to glare at the door as if he wants to run after the DJ.

The first guard's eyes widen as he turns to his co-worker, his face paling. Clearly not good news.

But my mentor is all over the gossip, his head cocks to the side as if he's using telepathy to listen in.

Rude, but effective. Until I met Smythe, I could only use telepathy to talk to T. Smythe can telepathically eavesdrop on almost anyone, either as a side effect of being a mage or as an inborn gift; he won't tell me which one. Luckily for me, he taught me mental barriers to keep him out of my mind.

Unfortunately, the guard had no such practice, his mind becoming an open book to Smythe's prying.

Smythe turns to me, his eyes wide.

They just found a woman's body by the Dumpster.

Chapter Two

"What?" The word slips out before I can stop it. But loose lips happen when shock and surprise strike. Smythe narrows his eyes, and I press my lips together. No sense in giving away our telepathic ability. *Sorry. You mean here?*

Where else would the stadium security mean?

Right, right. That's awful. Was she killed?

He doesn't know.

Sympathy for the woman and her family fill my thoughts. What happened? Was she killed, or did she kill herself? I hate hearing about dead women found in suspicious circumstances.

The two security guards hustle from the room, neither giving us a glance, unaware of Smythe's telepathic eavesdropping. Donny stares after them, his fingers fisting, clearly still thinking of Crazy Larry.

We need to go check it out. Smythe's voice snaps my attention from Donny to him.

You think it's a minion attack? Minions tend to hide their victims in or around Dumpsters. Not too original, but a help for us when trying to decide which crime scenes to investigate.

It has the Dumpster marking. Could just be a junkie who overdosed.

I suppose you mean to leave now? I haven't gotten an autograph.

Do you really want to see if Crazy Larry escapes the guards and returns to get his ass beat?

Good point. Let's go.

I glance around the room while Smythe heads to the door. Fans stand in line for autographs, music blares, and beer flows like the set of *Animal House*. Jackie tugs on Donny's shirt, pen in her hand, but his gaze focuses on me and heat rushes down my spine. I give him a little finger wave and mouth the words, *Gotta go.* He takes a step forward as if to stop me, but Jackie grabs his arm, stepping into his path. A flash of anger dances through his dark irises before he drops his attention to her pen and paper, a smile curving his lips.

One last thing to do before following Smythe. Let my twin know where I'm going.

T, we have to check something out.

His head snaps up from where he watches Donny scrawl his autograph on Jackie's paper. *Can't you ever just have a night off?*

Apparently not. I shrug. *We'll be back. Don't leave without us.*

As if he could. I'm driving.

Smythe holds the door open for me, and I slip into the relative quietness of the hallway. Not a soul around—at least not one I can see—but the rumbling bass of the party's stereo beats in the background.

"Where is everyone?"

Smythe gestures to the left as he quicksteps that direction. "The guards went through this exit door." He shoves the bar on the door, and lucky for us, no alarms sound.

We step into the humid, early fall evening. The scent of rain rides the breeze, overpowered by the odor

14

of trash and death. We stand in an enclosed alley-like area with an opened steel gate at the end. A large, green Dumpster sits to our left against a stretch of concrete wall, a bright LED light shining on the thing as if to make it easier to find in the dark. Or deter thieves from stealing it. A huddle of security and janitorial staff cluster around the Dumpster. Sirens wail in the distance, growing closer.

As the door clicks closed behind us, a couple of the closest security guards turn their attention our way.

"Hey, hey…" One of them walks toward us, palms out in the classic stop-right-there pose. "You can't be here. You need to—"

Smythe sets his laptop backpack on the ground by the door and pulls out what looks like a wallet. He flashes his fake badge, spelling the guard into thinking we are the local law enforcement. Mage power to the rescue. "FBI. Agent Smythe and Consultant Crawford. What happened?"

The guard's eyes lose focus for a second as the spell affects him. He waves us toward the scene, speaking to the others, who stare at us with curiosity. "They're with the FBI. Were at the game, heard about the crime."

Did Smythe implant that last idea? Or was that pure assumption on the guard's part?

I'll never tell. Smythe offers me a half-smile before slipping on his all-business face.

Wait a minute. Did he just read my mind? Before I can question him, he glances past the guard, his next words both a warning and a command. *Look smart.*

As if I won't. We've been through same type of scene numerous times. *Smart is my middle name.*

Smart as in sharp. Not as in smartass.

I shake my head at him before straightening my shoulders. And slapping a hand over my mouth and nose. Yuck. Hours-old death in humid Texas weather makes for a smelly situation. At least I'm not the only one with their hand, or handkerchief, over their mouths.

"What happened?" Smythe meets the gaze of each guard and the hyperventilating janitorial women who clearly found the body.

One of the women points to where the body lies in front of the Dumpster, flat on her back, hands resting in classic death pose on her bloody stabbed chest, a red rose clasped in her fingers. Her open eyes stare into the night, her mouth curled into a grimace of pain and death. Her clothes look like she came from a club: tight, short, and low-cut, with spiky heels. At one time, I would've been jealous of her hot-to-trot figure.

Now all I notice is the pain and terror stamped on her face and the unfurling anger deep in my core. Fucking murderers. I might be a fancy-assed demon huntress, but I destroy minions, not human killers. Lucky for me, I can tell which type of kill this scene belongs to with little effort.

Closing my eyes, I start to take a deep calming breath, think better of it, and focus on activating my minion sensors. Tapping into the power of the entity lying along my nerves, I open my eyes to a tactical grid display of reds and oranges, a clear indication of a minion's presence at the scene.

Looks like I'll get my wish to annihilate the fucking bastard who killed this poor woman.

Minion, I tell Smythe. Not that he needs the verbal—or should I say telepathic—heads-up. Mages can see minion trails just fine without a *Justitian's* help. Which makes me wonder why they need *Justitians.*

A topic for a different time.

"Brought the trash out and found this—" *This* hitches in the janitor's throat, cutting off the rest of her sentence, and she swallows as she waves at the body.

"What time was that?" Smythe asks.

The woman looks at her co-worker before answering. "Ten, fifteen minutes ago?"

"Did you come out earlier?"

Both women shake their heads, but only one answers. "No, señor. Only bring out trash after the game."

The sirens grow closer, an ear-piercing wail of sorrow. Flashing lights strobe across the walls of the stadium as the cops and an ambulance pull to a stop by the steel doors, the wail cutting off with an electronic blip. Smythe steps out of the headlights' glare.

Someone behind me draws in a sharp intake of air. Behind me?

I turn, the minion-sensors streaming red and orange minion trails like headlights in time-lapse photography. Donny Football stands a few feet behind me, staring at the dead woman, eyes wide, mouth open. The streams of minion trails coalesce around his head, across his shoulders, a lover's caress of evil.

Now it's my turn to gasp and blink in surprise. If he's a minion, why didn't my bracelet turn into a sword when we first met at the party? But as soon as I blink, the colors vanish, leaving Donny bathed in hues of blues and reds from the flashing strobe lights of the emergency vehicles.

Must've been a trick of the strobe lights. Clearly

Donny is not a minion. My *justitia* remains in bracelet form. A puzzled bracelet, but that emotion could be from my second of shock. No sword, no minion, I always say.

Good thing too. Thinking of Donny as a minion sends seeds of panic pumping through my system. Killing the football star would put me on everyone's hit list.

"I came to find you," Donny says. "What's going on?"

He came to find me? Me? Before I think too much into that phrasing, I show him what he wants, moving aside so he has a clear view.

He takes a step closer, his gaze never leaving the body. "Jenny?"

Jenny? He knows the dead woman?

Everyone stares at Donny like they've never seen the wide receiver off the field. Smythe recovers first, striding to him, eyes narrowed.

"Jenny, you say? How do you know her?"

"What, man? Like you're the cops?"

"Wrong department." Smythe flashes his badge. Open, close, and Donny believes we're an FBI agent and consultant. "Now. How do you know her?"

Donny swallows and runs a hand across his head. His gaze bounces from Jenny to the approaching emergency responders to Smythe. "Met her the other night at the club."

"Which one?"

"Club Monster."

"What's her last name?"

"Don't know." Donny shrugs. "Didn't get that far."

"When did you last see her?"

"She stayed at the club. Didn't leave with me."

"Did you meet with her outside of the club?"

"No, man. I don't take home women. Ruins my rep, ya know?"

Uh-huh. Right. Leaves the women at the club. Liar.

"I'm sorry." Bracing myself for emotional impact, I touch his arm as if to offer condolences.

He turns toward me, but his expression isn't what hits me. Moans, groans, and the rhythmic slapping of half-naked bodies slams into my mind, along with a graphic description of what Jenny feels like from the inside. Bleh, I could've done without that little glimpse of bathroom sex in a club.

Why take a woman home when he could bang her and leave her with no repercussions?

I'm surprised he remembered her name. Most men wouldn't.

I drop my arm while plastering a sympathetic expression on my face.

Smythe tenses like a lion ready to strike. Then he gives a little shudder and nods. "So you left her at the club and haven't seen her since?"

"Yeah, man. And before you ask, she was alive when I left. Very much alive."

"Did she say where she was going afterward?"

"Nah. Nothing like that. We didn't talk like that."

Why talk when "fuck me" and "bathroom" are uttered in the same sentence?

I've done a lot of things in my life better left unsaid, but bathroom sex in a club was not one of them.

"I see," Smythe says, stealing my line. His brain is blissfully ignorant of what Jenny feels like on the inside and the sound she makes when she peaks. Unlike mine.

19

I shake my head, as if that will disperse the feeling. Whoever thinks being an empath is fun should try randomly touching people's arms. That'll cure 'em.

Squeaky wheels and heavy footsteps draw closer as the emergency responders swarm the scene. Chatter fills the air, a dull hum of jaded remorse. See enough bodies and one stops empathizing with the dead as a coping mechanism.

Smythe rests his hand against Donny's shoulder, almost as if he wants to play empath and read the football star's emotions. Which is a little hard to do without touching skin-to-skin.

"Give your statement to the cops." He points to the nearest blue-suit, gesturing the cop to Donny. Then he steps back, giving me a little tug. Unlike Donny, his touch elicits no empathic reading.

No complaints about that. When we first started working together his touch sent zingers of do-me-now heat straight to my core. For whatever reason, those rarely happen nowadays. Good thing too. The mage turns me on without the addition of my touch-and-feel problem. Which makes keeping my rule of "Thou shalt not screw thy boss" difficult.

Once the cops invade our space, Smythe tugs me backward until we run into the stadium door. Escape mage-style.

"What? Don't want to meet the cops?"

"Why mingle when I can look up the case online?" He picks up his laptop backpack from where he laid it next to the door.

Right. The spell-protected laptop. No hacker's getting through that thing.

"We aren't tracking the minion?" Minion trails

only last about a day before dissipating into the air. Smythe usually insists upon immediate tracking.

"We'll have to come back tomorrow when it's not so crowded."

"But won't that be too late?"

"For what?" He gestures toward Jenny. "She's already dead."

"You usually like to get a head start."

"There's a time for everything, and right now is not it. Come on, let's go."

Fine by me. It's late. I'm tired, and despite wanting to catch Jenny's killer, I'd rather catch a nighttime of zzz's.

Smythe pulls open the door and we step into the cool air of the hallway. Nothing screams North Texas like over-air-conditioned buildings.

"Where did you go?"

The door hasn't even shut behind us when T steps into my space. Like he couldn't pop into my head and see for himself. Maybe barriers to keep Smythe out of my head and my secrets work on my twin.

Nah. After thirty-two years, I know what he's up to. Concern works better up close and personal.

"Minion kill. Was Donny Merryweather's flavor du jour." I point at the door.

T's jaw tenses. He doesn't like my new demon-killing gig. On the plus side, he now likes my mentor.

T narrows his eyes at Smythe. "She shouldn't be running around looking at dead people when we're at a game."

Okay. Make that still learning to like my mentor. The word "like" being used loosely and only when Smythe toes T's treat-my-sister-right line.

Dead bodies and minion kills lie on the other side of that divide.

Smythe stares at T until my twin blinks. Which has to be the first time in T's adult life he's backed down.

"Okay, okay, guys." No sense in letting them think playing the stare-and-glare game wins friends and influences people. "I'm the newest demon huntress—"

"*Justitian,*" Smythe mutters.

"—and nothing's going to stop me from doing my job. I take down minions, and I'm damn good at it."

"Doesn't mean I have to like it."

"I know." I touch T's arm and tension leaks from him, a slow drip of anger replaced by relaxation. A mutual feeling for both of us, a peace only found from the touch of the other.

Yeah, it's not just our names, Gin Champagne and Tonic Scotch, that make us the poster children for not drinking during pregnancy.

"Think you can talk to the dead woman's ghost?" Smythe asks the question with all sincerity, as if he forgot T refuses to use his ghost-talking abilities. Ever since that time when we were teenagers and used a ghost's help to get rid of our abusive father, T does everything in his power to avoid ghosts. Including any mention of the see-through buggers.

T's jaw tenses hard enough to pop as he takes a step away from me. "I. Don't. Talk. To. Them."

"You said you'd think about it."

"I had a weak moment."

The weak moment named Eloise.

"Have another one. See if you can talk to her ghost." Smythe tilts his head in the direction of the door.

T's fingers flex open and closed, open and closed, as his nostrils flare. Air thickens around him as if his anger coalesces into matter.

Then he shakes his head and draws in a deep breath. A heavy sigh later and he steps to the door, shoves it open, and pauses. His shoulders sag as he pulls the door shut.

"Ain't no ghost out there. Either it's already fled, or she didn't die here."

"Didn't take you long to look."

I glare at Smythe. "If he said there was no ghost, then there's no ghost. No ghost means no talking to it. Your hacking skills are up next."

Defending T is second nature. Believing him is an entirely different matter. I don't have to hop into his head to know he lied.

He'd kept his eyes closed when he opened the door.

"He's right about one thing," Smythe says. "She didn't die here."

Chapter Three

Say what? But then my mind wanders back to scene, to the lack of blood under the woman, despite multiple stab wounds. She'd clearly been arranged; most people don't grasp flowers as they die.

Why? What kind of freak were we dealing with?

Well, duh, a minion. Demons picked their minions well. Most of the walking evil flunked out of law-abiding school. Selling their soul to a demon in exchange for super strength and the ability not to age appealed to a lot of people. Why bank on an eternal life floating around in the clouds with a harp when you can have everything now?

"How do you know that?" T's brows draw together, snapping my attention to the conversation.

"Lack of blood." Smythe fists his hand over his heart. "And did you see how she held that rose?"

"She was holding a rose?" Surprise laces my twin's voice as his eyes flare. "That's creep-ass weird."

"The killer arranged the scene." Check me out, all down with proper terms and shit.

"I agree." Smythe nods. "People don't tend to lie down, let someone stab them, then pick up a rose before dying. I'll check the police database once we get back to the house."

"Where's Jackie?" Luckily she's not in the hall overhearing a conversation about Donny Football's dead booty call. Might kill her enthusiasm for the wide receiver.

No pun intended.

"Still at the party." T's jaw clenches. "Going crazy over meeting the guys and getting autographs."

"Why'd you leave?" Smythe starts walking toward the party suite, T and I following.

"Got tired of watching Jackie ogle the players. Thought y'all might be having more fun." T yanks open the door, releasing music and conversation at a volume pitched more for a rock concert than a meet-and-greet. "That'll teach me for thinking."

He strides into the middle of the party, leaving Smythe and me on the periphery. After seeing Jenny stabbed, being all perky and awestruck isn't in my playbook. Her death reminds me of Blake's, killed by one of Hell's denizens. But unlike my lover, she died from a minion's hand, not a demon's.

Heaviness settles in my chest, a remembrance of what was, a knowledge of what could have been, what will never be. Grief pulls around me like a cloak, and I shrug it off. I no longer cry myself to sleep, guilt creeping across my skin like spiders, but Blake's loss sticks with me, striking at unexpected moments.

Smythe places a hand on my shoulder, gives a little squeeze.

How did he know? I don't notice him in my mind. Maybe it's some sort of mage trick. Or he's good at reading body language.

I draw in a deep breath and straighten my spine. Appearances are everything. I can tear up in the privacy of my bedroom.

Provided T manages to remove an inebriated, star-struck Jackie from the party.

****

Jackie talks the entire way home, a play-by-play of who signed an autograph for her, what they looked like, and how she wouldn't mind fucking Donny Football, no offense T.

I don't have to take my eyes off the road to know my twin is offended. His anger strokes against my skin, but the most he'd do to the clueless blonde is break up with her. In the morning. Because he might as well have one last hoorah before jumping on the not-getting-any wagon.

The power of double-D's. They turn an otherwise intelligent man into a simpering, sex-crazed idiot.

By the time I pull into the garage, I'm ready for some shut eye, STAT. It's late, past midnight, but at least I'm working a swing shift and don't have to report to the ER until 3 p.m. tomorrow, make that today. T stalks Jackie into the house, Smythe and I following. The snap of his bedroom door shuts off her incessant chattering.

Thank God.

I grab a glass of water as Smythe strides to the living room. Squeaking couch springs announce his landing place.

I swallow the water in one long gulp, put the glass on the counter, and turn to face him. "I'm going to bed."

"I'm going to see if there's any info on the department's website." He pulls his laptop out of the backpack and pops it open, speaking to the screen. "Won't take long. They probably don't have much up yet."

"Enjoy." I waggle my fingers good night, and he returns the wave without glancing away from his computer.

Finally. I can relax, push the night's activity out of my head, and go to sleep. Plenty of time to track down the minion tomorrow.

I step into my room, close the door, and flip on the light. And come to a heart-pounding stop. Sweat shimmies down my spine. A sinking heaviness settles in my lower belly.

Zagan, the demon of lies and deceit, sprawls on my bed, jean-clad legs crossed at the ankles, head resting on his hands, his biceps bunching in a mouth-watering manner. A tight, white t-shirt frames his muscular chest and abs, pulls tight around his arms. Hot as hell and just as freaking scary.

Instead of turning into a sword and showing the demon who's boss, my stupid *justitia* jitters the happy-happy joy-joy dance on my wrist. The malfunctioning bracelet considers Zagan a friend.

And what does my esteemed employer, the Agency, have to say about that? My favorite line: *justitias don't have friends.*

Uh-huh. Tell that to my bracelet.

I have my suspicions of how their friendship started: Zagan created the bracelet. But why? And how was it turned into a demon-killing entity? One day I'll figure out the whole story of their relationship. When the sexy demon isn't lying on my bed.

He props on one elbow as he turns to face me, a smile breaking across his face as his gaze rakes me from head to toe and back. Straight white teeth gleam in an olive-toned face, no evidence of his abnormally sharp tongue seen behind his firm lips. I shiver away the memory of his tongue slicing through mine when we shared a kiss. Soulless black eyes twinkle as he stretches out a hand toward me. "Hello, Gin."

My name rolls off his tongue in that ancient Middle Eastern accent of his, and it's not a shiver of fear skating across my skin. *Damn it.*

I ignore his hand. Last time I touched him skin-on-skin my brain almost hemorrhaged. "What are you doing in my room, Zagan?"

"Why this"—he waves his hand between us— "animosity? Can friends not sit around and talk?"

"Sure. But we're not friends."

He drops his hand and pushes to a sit. "Nonsense. I help you. You help me. That is the human definition of friendship, yes?"

"Not exactly." I refuse to debate the intricacies of friendship with one of Hell's denizens. "Want to tell me why you're here?"

He clucks his tongue. "Patience, little *Justitian*, patience."

I lean against the door, cross my arms, and try to look nonchalant. Or as nonchalant as one can be when faced with a demon. I'm pretty sure he won't eat me, kill me, or flambé my ass. Which still leaves a wide range of other harmful possibilities.

Along with some not-so-harmful ones.

I will not look frightened. I do not fear the big, bad, sexy demon. I definitely don't want him to realize he simultaneously terrifies and turns me on. Each time he appears, my emotional response confuses the hell out of me. Which results in me acting nonchalant so he won't catch on. Fake it 'til you make it.

One side of his lips kicks up, as if he reads my thoughts. Which he can't do. Right? God, I hope that's right. His ability to port into my room unannounced is bad enough.

"Nasty murder tonight, was it not?"

Nonchalant no longer, I push away from my relaxed pose, eyes wide. "How did you know about that?"

"Hell is full of gossips. And observers. Perhaps I can help you."

"Let me get this straight. You, a demon, would help me, a *Justitian*, catch a killer?"

"You sound surprised." His eyebrows rise in fake shock as if he actually thinks I wouldn't question his aid.

As a rule, demons and *Justitians* fight each other, not hold hands and join a crime-stopping brigade. Although, in the past, Zagan gave me a clue about how to defeat a demon. It took me awhile to understand his cryptic message, but in the end I killed the demon of fear. Sent its scaly ass to Hell where the creature can rot for all eternity.

Go me.

"Damn straight. I thought demons were all about killing and maiming and creating minions."

"Killing is passé—"

"And yet you killed Jezebeth." Right before the crazy bitch demon tried to kill me. Right after she killed Blake. I shove the memories aside and focus on the present.

He shrugs. "I said passé, not unnecessary. Sometimes killing is the only option. But resolving differences through debate and persuasion is much less bloody, yes?"

"Isn't killing a type of persuasion?"

He chuckles. "I believe the word you want is torture, not killing. But we could argue the point all night. See, debate. Works well, does it not?"

"Your point?" One thing I've learned about Zagan, he always has a point. Discovering that point is a whole other matter.

"Patience. I will give you what you need, but you might already have the answers."

A thought niggles my brain. He knows. Gossip in Hell, my foot. "You know who killed that woman we found tonight, don't you?"

"Ah-ha. There's my *Justitian.* Yes."

"Who?"

"A jealous minion."

"Okay. Can you be a little more specific?"

His eyes narrow. "That is specific."

Right. "Okay, then. Thank you."

He nods. "Remember our friendship. Remember I gave you a part of me, a part of my power."

A power he buried deep inside me without telling me. Not that I'm complaining. I killed the fear demon Agramon with the red energy Zagan gave me. But why would a demon give a *Justitian* power to slay another demon?

Something to think on later. I need all my faculties to deal with Zagan.

"Why did you give it to me?"

One brow raises as he ignores my question. "Use it wisely. Soon a time will come when you will need it again. Be prepared. And remember, I am here. If you need me. But you already know that, don't you?" He stands, steps toward me until he stands inches from my refusing-to-move body. He places the palm of his hand against my chest, over my heart. He leans forward, lips inches away from my ear, his breath warm against my skin. "I am always with you, always a part of you. *Friends.*"

His words send chills racing across my skin, through my veins, equal doses of fear and arousal. He steps back, lifts his palm to the ceiling, circles his hand, and winks as a portal swallows him.

I sag against the door, knees unwilling to support me, my body sinking to the floor. On the plus side, he didn't kill me. On the minus side, he thinks we're friends.

It could be worse. I could be his human servant.

Only by a trick of my *justitia* did I manage to avoid that fate. How was I supposed to know that giving a demon food and some of my blood meant I was bound to them as their servant? In my defense, I figured giving the big bad demon crackers to snack on instead of me was the way to go. Faulty thinking there.

Zagan somehow left his mark on me. A rune denoting his name tattooed into my neck behind my ear. He claims I belong to him, always have, always will.

I say whatever, demon. I'm not going down the human servant route without a fight. *Bring. It. On.*

Then he appears in my bedroom, and all that bravado disappears like water vapor. Part of me wants him, most of me fears him.

Friendship, my ass.

His visit means I need to tell my mentor. After screwing things up between us by tricking an Agency attack force into believing I killed Zagan, which violated our tender thread of trust, I promised Smythe I'd let him know when Zagan visited me. For the most part, I've stuck to that promise.

Even if it means a long conversation when I really want to go to sleep.

The things I do to keep evil at bay.

Chapter Four

I shove to a stand and open the door. A dull clack of fingers typing on a keyboard echoes through the house punctuated by the age-old rhythm of T's headboard thumping against the living room wall. How Smythe works with that racket, I'll never understand.

Maybe he conjured up a pair of noise-dampening earplugs.

I cut through the kitchen to avoid walking past T's door.

"Hey, Smythe."

Thump, thump, thump.

Smythe looks at me, his fingers taking a break from the laptop. He glances to the rattling wall and shakes his head at the sounds turning my living room into a soundtrack from a porno set.

"Thought you were going to bed."

"Something happened."

He sets his laptop on the coffee table and walks into the kitchen. "What's wrong?"

This time the touch of his hand on my arm elicits a tingling response, lightning firing low and spreading outward. I swallow.

"Zagan paid me a visit."

"What?" His hand drops, but the lightning continues to fire through my veins.

Damn hormones.

"He was waiting in my room."

"This whole time you've been talking to him?"

"Pretty much. Yes."

His eyes narrow before he strides to the couch. He picks up his cell phone, carrying it back to the kitchen, each step punctuated by a wall-rattling *thump, thump, thump*.

T really needs to move out.

I stand beside Smythe as he dials a number and slams the phone against his ear hard enough to give a normal person a headache.

"Do you have a record of a demon appearance in Peterstown, Texas?…No? Are you sure the program is working correctly?…Uh-huh…Yes, I know it doesn't always work, but this demon keeps appearing and it never verifies him. Uh-huh…Well, maybe someone should work harder to fix the problem." His finger stabs the end button, and he slaps the phone against his thigh. "Same problem. The program picked up a demon appearance in the Middle East earlier this evening so in their eyes, the damn thing works just fine. Clearly it's malfunctioning."

I shrug. Do computers ever work right all the time? I'm still impressed a program exists to track demon appearances on Earth. Past experience with the demon identification program doesn't surprise me it failed to pick up Zagan. Come to think of it, has the thing ever picked up my visiting demon? Do I want it to?

"Okay." Smythe slaps the phone twice against his leg as if that makes him think better. "We need to learn how Zagan avoids the program. He's here for longer than the thirty seconds required to log a demon's presence, so what's he doing to escape notice?"

Clearly I'm not catching my zzz's until Smythe reaches a solution. Which means I need to offer a possibility, STAT. I rub my forehead, hoping the motion releases an answer. "The program only tracks when demons appear from Hell, since their appearance causes a rupture in the space-time continuum. Maybe he's not going back to Hell. Maybe he stays on Earth. Maybe he still lives in his lair."

"Too many maybes." Smythe shakes his head and slams a hand against the counter. "We need answers. Why are you important to him?"

"Hello." Talk about an easy answer. I point at my neck, at the rune symbolizing Zagan. "Because of this, he thinks I'm his servant."

"But you're not." The slight inflection at the end of the sentence sounds like he's questioning my loyalty.

A twinge squeezes my chest. I don't blame Smythe for questioning where my loyalties lie, but it hurts nonetheless. Two months ago, I helped Zagan with an illusion, allowing him to escape while the Agency thought he died. Needless to say, my actions angered Smythe and caused a rift between us, a rift filled with broken trust.

A bit of that trust was restored when I saved Smythe's life during a fight with a badass demon. A little hard to doubt my loyalties then. I'd do almost anything for my mentor. The Agency? Well, that's a whole other matter. Trust for my employer wavers between nonexistent and barely there.

I force myself to look Smythe in the eye, to not flinch from the anger drifting in the depths of his gaze, to let him see the truth behind my words. "He does not control me."

Smythe nods, relief flashing across his face before he slips on his mask of resolve. Nope, definitely not going to bed anytime soon.

"What did he want?"

"To tell me he knew who killed Jenny and I might know too."

"Did he kill her?"

"No, he said a jealous minion did it."

Smythe pauses before nodding. "Leaving her with a rose isn't something he'd do. Come to think of it, that's not what any demon would do. At least not a demon I know of."

I yawn, a subtle indication this conversation needs to wrap up sooner rather than later.

Smythe ignores my silent plea. "Minion kill then. So why leave the body at the stadium? Why not leave her where she was killed?"

"To make a point?" Since the subtle failed, I move on to the obvious. "I'm sleepy. Think we can finish this discussion in the morning?"

He looks at me as if seeing into my soul, his gaze leaving a hot trail of interest as he searches my face. "Sorry. I should've noticed." He touches my arm, a brief stroke of his fingers before he drops his hand.

Heat pools warm against my skin, in my blood, a pulling of need. I meet his heated gaze. He swallows. I lick my lips. His hand cups my cheek as he steps closer. My heart pounds against my ribs as I tilt my face to his.

In slow motion, his head bends toward me. Firm lips cover mine, and I melt into a kiss missing the clatter of another's emotions storming my mind. I love it. I can't get enough of his quiet touch.

I wrap my arms around his neck and run my tongue

across the seam of his lips. He responds with a moan low in his throat, a vibration of pleasure rumbling from his chest into mine.

THUMP! "Oh baby, yes, yes, yes!" Jackie's shrill orgasmic voice cuts right through our moment, a big bucket of cold water thrown onto a raging brushfire.

Smythe steps back, red tingeing his cheeks. He opens his lips and closes them as if he wants to speak but the words stick in his mouth. Stupid Jackie and her enthusiastic response to horizontal action. I swear, this is T's last night in my house. My almost extracurricular activity ruined by a double-D blonde bimbo.

Although maybe I should thank my twin for keeping me from breaking the eleventh commandment of Gin: no messing around with thy boss.

I glance at my mentor, at his muscular six-foot-five physique, at the seriousness in his blue eyes. Remember the way he's always there for me, his friendship, his breakfast making skills. On second thought, who pays attention to commandments?

Smythe clears his throat. "That was awkward."

It could be worse. He could apologize for kissing me. Instead he speaks the truth. In more ways than one. "Yeah."

"I can usually tune them out."

"Seriously?" I raise a brow. "How the hell do you do that?"

He shrugs. Mysterious mage powers to the rescue. "I just do." He offers me a half smile, his gaze centering on my lips, a banked fire of lust behind his eyes. "Gin…"

"Yeah?" my voice purrs, all hope mingled with sexiness.

"You look dead on your feet. Why don't you go to sleep, and I'll see if the detectives have made a case report. We'll meet up in the morning and return to the Dumpster. See if we can find anything new."

"Right." So much for hoping for a different ending.

Instead of carrying out my fantasies, he's formulating a game plan. Not that I blame him. Avoidance of prickly emotions has been my modus operandi for so long it's like pulling on a comfy pair of socks. "Good night, Smythe."

I'm to the door of my bedroom before his voice stops me.

"Gin?"

I look over my shoulder. "Yeah?"

"I'm not sorry."

With those words, he strides into the living room, leaving me alone with nothing for comfort except my battery-operated BFF and a wishful imagination.

Chapter Five

Bright sunlight streams through a crack in the blinds, forcing me awake. The scent of bacon mixed with coffee draws my eyes open. *Mmmm.* Bacon and coffee. A great start to any morning.

Even mornings when you'd rather stay in bed.

The clock reads 9:00 in glowing red numbers. I blink in surprise. Smythe let me sleep in? Is he sick?

Curiosity and hunger propel me out of bed. Fifteen minutes and a shower later, my feet follow the aroma of breakfast into the kitchen. Smythe stands in front of the stove, the sizzle of bacon releasing a strong allure. But not nearly as strong as the fresh pot of coffee. My mentor makes a mean breakfast.

Since he looks as well as ever, I assume his allowing me to sleep in means he's turned into a kinder, gentler hard-ass.

Must be due to last night's kiss. Not that I'm going to mention what could have been without Jackie's not-so-timely interruption. Not unless he brings it up first. And the chances of that happening are about as likely as two feet of snow in North Texas. "Morning." I pull my extra-large mug out of the cabinet and apply a dose of the liquid black gold to its insides. I might be able to move in the mornings without caffeine, but my personality tends to improve with each cup. Since Smythe wants to track minions today, I need to fuel up and transform from Madam Grumpy-pants into Ms. Nice Mentee.

Self-improvement via caffeine.

"The sleepyhead finally wakes."

I grunt a better-left-as-nonverbal reply while taking a sip of the tongue-burning liquid.

His lip twitches. "I heard that."

"What? I said something?" I force my eyes wide, all mock innocent.

"You said something, all right." He winks as he places a strip of bacon on a plate loaded with eggs.

Time for a topic change. "T and Jackie still in bed?"

He shakes his head while dropping two slices of bacon into the skillet. "They woke me up trying to be quiet leaving. I guess they're at work?"

I shrug. Damn. Looks like once again sex and double D's conned T into staying in the relationship. Men and their fascination with boobs.

"Work, yeah, it's Friday." Little caffeine particles finally make their way into my brain, flickering on neurons. "Sorry, as you know, mornings aren't my thing."

"Never would've guessed."

I roll my eyes. "We still hitting the minion trail?"

"Yep." He flips a piece of bacon onto the plate and hands it to me. "Eat up. You've slept half the morning."

"Hey, it's my morning off. I'm allowed." I take the plate and my mug and walk to the table. His words follow me, small stalkers of guilt.

"Not when there's a minion to track."

This time I ignore him. In the three months we've been working together, I've learned to track minions as quick as most people process thoughts. What's a little shut-eye when I can track down the walking evil in no time flat?

Minions, here I come.

Right after I read the paper and eat my breakfast. I spread out the newspaper—thank you, whoever plopped it on the table for me—and pop a bite of bacon into my mouth. Yummy. My favorite, cooked through but not crispy. Smythe's skills with a skillet and a spatula rank high on my list of things I love about the man. If only he lived here on a permanent basis and not just when he needed to crash.

Did I actually think that? I glance up at my mentor as he places the last pieces of bacon on his plate.

Smythe sits across from me, his brows twitching together. "What?"

"What, what?" Yeah, right. Like I'm actually going to tell him I want to fuck his brains out. He might take me up on it.

Or worse, he might not.

"You had a strange look."

"Just planning my day." I'm such a good little liar. "You find anything on the report?"

He stares at me for a two count before his brow relaxes. He nods. "She didn't die by the Dumpster."

"Newsflash, we already knew that." I swallow a couple of gulps of the no longer burn-your-tongue-hot coffee, trying to get as much caffeine in my system as fast as possible. Past experience taught me when Smythe falls into minion-hunting mode, caffeine becomes a rare commodity. The man thinks my mug is optional on hunts. You'd think by now he'd realize never to come between a grumpy woman and her morning addiction.

"Just confirming. They also gave the body a last name. Jenny O'Connor."

Nothing about my touch-n-see episode with Donny gave me her full name. Speaking of, maybe I should fess up about what I saw.

"I touched Donny last night."

"You didn't say anything."

"It was…" I squeeze my eyes shut and shudder at the memory. "…unpleasant."

His eyes flare. "You saw him kill her?"

"Don't be ridiculous. We wouldn't be planning a minion hunt if that was the case."

"Right, right. Guess I'm not as awake as I thought."

"See?" I point a piece of bacon at him before popping it in my mouth and talking around it. Etiquette be damned. "That's what you get for calling me a sleepyhead."

He grins. "I can't help telling the truth." The smile fades from his face as his gaze grows serious. "What did you see when you touched Donny?"

"Them having sex in a club bathroom." My face twists involuntarily. "Gross. Do you know what's in those bathrooms?"

"Semen?"

"Well, that too, but yuck, all the germs."

"Was he telling the truth about leaving her at the club?"

"No clue. The only memory I saw was them"—I wave my hand—"in the bathroom. That was bad enough."

"So he could've lied."

"Killed her and then met up with a minion to dispose of her body? Then acted all shocked and surprised she was dead? I suppose. I could also win the lottery."

Smythe raises one brow. "Highly unlikely doesn't mean impossible. Remember that."

Through a strong application of willpower, I manage to avoid an eye roll. Go me. Instead, I circle my hand, encouraging him to keep talking. "Try for option number two. What else ya got?"

"The detectives are trying to determine who she was with at the club, so they can talk to her friends. I should have more information tonight."

"I work from three to eleven." Which means I probably won't leave work until midnight. Friday nights in an ER never end on time.

Smythe focuses on shoveling several bites of eggs into his mouth. Unlike me, he waits until after swallowing before speaking.

"We better get going then. It's almost ten. You having to work cuts into our time to track the minion."

What he fails to say, yet tinges his words with accusation, is how my working as an ER nurse goes against the Agency standards. No *Justitian* except me holds a job. How freaking plebian. A job. Why work when you were born into a wealthy cult that admits no new members? Not only do they not have to work, but unlike me, they all know their heritage and trained their entire life to be ready to fall into the role of demon huntress. I'm an oddity all the way around.

As if "odd" and "Gin Crawford" don't already go together.

You'd think when the *justitia* chose me to wear it,

the Agency would want to ante up and pay my bills, allowing me to work for them full-time. But no, come to find out, being appreciative of my services was not in their playbook. One of them, a blonde bitch named Samantha, tried to kill me for some unnamed reason and all of them see me as trailer-park trash.

Despite me never living in a trailer park.

Their attitude doesn't bother me. Not much anyway. I wear a *justitia*. I kill minions and the occasional demon. I rock. Who cares what they think? Without me, they would be missing a valuable *Justitian*.

Time to show off my abilities.

I shove my chair back and walk my mug and plate to the sink. "I'll take the second cup with me."

He chuckles, turning in his chair to face me. "As you wish. Just get a move on."

"Let me brush my teeth first, and I'll be right back."

I leave the mug on the counter and hustle to my bathroom for the toothbrush. Some might find following a minty fresh mouth with a cup of java disgusting, but I've grown used to the taste. Not much different than adding mint to chocolate and who doesn't like that concoction?

A few minutes later and I return to the kitchen, pour my second mug and salute Smythe with the cup. He shakes his head and sighs.

"Ready, padawan?"

You've gotta love a man who's as big a geek as you. I smile at his nickname for me. The reference never grows old in my book.

I take a sip of the coffee before answering. "Ready

as ever."

He holds out his hand, palm facing the wall, and speaks words in an ancient language that sounds suspiciously like Latin. A slash in the space-time continuum opens, deceptively warm air billowing outward, a portal from my house to the stadium. Much faster than driving. Smythe grabs my hand, and we walk into the cold depths of the portal. How the things manage to spit out warm air yet be colder than Antarctica makes it onto the world's most-amazing-oddities list.

When we step out of the portal beside the stadium Dumpster, my hands are a nice shade of eggplant and I shiver despite the warmth of the day. Steam no longer circles my mug. Smythe touches the mug, speaks a word, and steam once again flows out of the top. Mage power to the rescue.

Maybe I'll cut him some slack for not waiting until I had my third cup.

You'd better, drifts through my mind as he winks at me.

"Smythe, Smythe, Smythe. Reading minds without permission is rude." Especially my mind. Some things in there he never needs to know.

"It's not invasive if the thought's projected into my mind. I was answering your comment."

"You say po-tay-toe, I say bullshit. But it's all good." I pat his arm. "You heated my coffee."

He shakes his head and offers me a grin. "You have an addiction, you know."

"Hey, it's coffee. And it helps cover up the smell of the trash."

"Good point." His nose wrinkles. "Besides the

obvious, what do you see?"

I close my eyes and draw in a deep breath as I tap into the minion sensors in my eyes. When I first started as a demon huntress, using the phrase 'minion sensors in my eyes' struck me as crazy. As in, I expected little men in white suits to show up at any minute and haul my ass to Blue Shores, my hospital's psychiatric facility. Now? The phrase is as familiar to me as asking for a beer.

Guess that means I'm not going crazy after all.

When I open my eyes, red and red-orange lines streak around the narrow space, clearly coming from the steel doors at the end of the alley. The lines are thickest next to the Dumpster where Jenny's body was found. Usually a thick red line means the site of the crime, but in this case, it meant the minion hung out by her body for awhile.

So where did he kill her?

"The trails come from the doors and are thickest by the Dumpster."

"Good. That's what I see too." Smythe nods.

Mages see minion trails like *Justitians* do. Which begs the question of why they need us. The Agency claims that only the sword of the *justitia* possesses the ability to kill the essence of a demon. Demon essence imbues minions. In theory, if you kill enough minions with a *justitia,* the demon becomes weakened. While a mage can kill minions, they can't destroy the demon's essence hosted in a minion in such a way as to injure the demon. Hence the need for *Justitians.*

Sounds plausible, but something seems off to me. An idea niggles in the back of my brain, telling me another reason exists. Wouldn't surprise me at all to discover the Agency lies. Enough intrigue and unanswered questions exist in that place to give a thriller author plot lines for the rest of eternity.

Questions such as *Where do* justitias *come from?* and *Why are there only thirteen to fight all the demons and minions on the planet?* should have a quick response. But the esteemed Agency seems foggy on the answers.

"Hello, Gin." Smythe waves his hand in front of my face, snapping me out of my thoughts and back to the present.

Heat slaps my cheeks. "Sorry."

"Stay focused. What do you think happened?"

I narrow my eyes at him. "I am focused." Just not on the minion trails. One of these days I'm going to get my questions answered by someone other than Zagan. You know you have a problem if the demon of lies and deceit tells the truth more often than your employer. "I see the same thing you do. Minion carried the body in and lingered by it. Pride over his kill?"

Smythe shrugs. "Maybe. Or taking time to arrange the body. Either way, the minion lingered. Did it walk or drive?"

I head to the steel doors, following the minion trail. Instead of being locked, the doors are merely closed as if to make things easy for the garbage truck. Or a demon huntress and her guardian.

I push one door open only to jump back when the motion snaps apart the yellow crime-scene tape. Damn it. Should've realized the police had taped off the scene after CSI worked all night to discover clues.

Smythe peers over my shoulder at the tape damage. "Repairing the damage is outside my scope of magic."

"Let me get this straight. You can heat my coffee, but not repair tape?"

"Magic should not be used for such minor things. The coffee was a necessity, not a minor thing."

Nice to know he finally understands my coffee addiction. Not so nice to know he won't erase evidence we tampered with a crime scene.

The chances of the police catching us are slim to none. Fuzzing out cameras is an ability of Smythe's he doesn't mind using. Speaking of…

"Do you see a camera?" I point to the stadium. "You don't suppose we were seen appearing, do you?"

Smythe's brow raise subs in for speech. Right. He clearly already thought of it, which makes me seem like a nag.

"I took care of the camera while you were looking for the minion trail."

"Sorry. I shouldn't have asked."

He makes a noncommittal noise. "Looks like the minion arrived in a car. You see that?" He shoves the steel door wider and steps through, pointing at a spot on the concrete several feet in front of us.

A bright blood-red splotch of minion activity hovers above the concrete of the parking lot, a stain of evil. Still strong despite the lapse of time. Most minion trails disappear after about twenty-four hours and start fading after twelve. This one looks as fresh as if made an hour ago.

Creepy.

"Why does it look so fresh?"

"Not sure." He pauses, staring at the stain. "Maybe it's more evil than most."

"That's scarier than Agramon." I shiver at the fear

demon's name. I fought it and won, but barely. That creature was one scary-ass demon, the likes of whom I hope never to see again.

"Not quite." Smythe shakes his head, negating the possibility of anything scarier than a fear demon.

A frisson of relief skates along my veins.

"Okay, then. At any rate, the minion parked here and left the body. No clue why. And because it drove, I don't see where it came from or where it went."

"Yeah." Smythe crosses his arms, eyeing the red splotch of minion activity as if it spoke all the answers.

Which it didn't. At least not any I heard.

"Hey, think you can do that magic mojo and drop us into wherever the minion is now?"

On my first minion hunt, we tracked a minion to its house where it promptly hopped in a car and drove hell-bent for the Texas-Oklahoma border. Smythe cast a spell and portaled us right into the minion's moving car. We almost died before managing to kill the minion. At the time, I swore never again, but if it would help find Jenny's killer, I can break my vow.

"The trail is too old. That spell only works with a fresh trail. We have to hunt this minion the old-fashioned way."

I clear my throat to keep my sarcastic remark buried inside my mouth. At least the day was overcast and in the upper sixties. Unlike other old-fashioned minion hunts where I about sweated my skin off. Texas heat and walking outside make for a poor mix.

"Let's go." Smythe gestures toward the Dumpster. "There's nothing else we can do here."

"Go where?"

He pulls his phone out of his back pocket and looks

at the time. "Back to your place. Maybe they've updated the police report."

Chapter Six

The police have not updated the report. Either the detectives were slow thinkers, or they put in all their notes at the end of the day. Neither option puts Smythe in his happy place. And while I could think up a suitable activity guaranteed to put a smile on his face, the end result would be confusion coupled with more talking things through than it's worth.

Hence the grumpy mentor sitting on my couch when I leave for work, his fingers drumming a rhythm against his leg. His "later" follows me out the door.

The drive to work takes no time since traffic waits until the four o'clock hour to strike. Dallas: the city where more time is spent sitting in traffic than out of traffic and rush hour lasts from four to seven.

The ER hums a busy tune as I duck into the break room and store my purse in my locker. The break room door opens as I twirl the dial on the lock. When I turn, Will Wunderliech, M.D. stands frozen two steps inside, an "oh shit" expression on his face, as if I was the last person he wanted to see.

As if? More like definite want on the avoidance. Ever since that day a couple of months ago when Smythe and I paid him a visit, informing him of his mage status, Will has gone out of his way to avoid me.

Part of me doesn't blame him. Who wants to find out you have hidden magic and now some secret freaky organization wants you to work for them? The other part of me hurts for our friendship. I've known Will since high school, when I was the school freak and he paid attention to me.

"Hey. How's it going?" Might as well be friendly until he works through everything and stops avoiding me.

His lips press together as he draws in a breath through his nose. "Gin."

"Coming or going?"

"Neither. I'm here until ten."

"Doing okay?" On the day I found my *justitia*, Will was shot by a minion. If not for his latent mage abilities, which include quick healing, he'd be dead. A walking miracle, according to his doctors.

I know better.

He shrugs. After shooting him, the minion killed Will's wife. All for my bracelet, which Will had possessed prior to giving it to me. Not that he remembers giving it to me, but he had to have. How else would the thing have appeared in my scrub pocket?

"That guy you introduced me to isn't around, is he?" His eyes narrow on a spot to the side of me, as if he expects Smythe to lurk behind the vending machine.

"Nope. He's at home."

"Hmm." Will nods but doesn't move. Except for his gaze, which darts everywhere but my face.

I sigh. "You gonna take Smythe up on his offer?"

"Don't know." The tick of the clock above the door counts the seconds of silence. "Not sure I want to travel that path."

"I understand." I nod. "Trust me. But sometimes we have to be what we are. Who we are deep inside.

You know?" Check me out, all philosophical and shit.

His gaze snaps to mine, hurt mingling with anger. "Are you living what you are deep inside, Gin? Are you?"

Heat rushes out of my cheeks fast enough to make the room spin. Does he know my secret? Does he know what I am deep inside is not the pretty package I portray to the world?

But he's no longer looking at me. Will yanks the door open and storms off, his white coat flapping behind him.

The door snaps closed, and I release a breath of air I didn't realize I held. He's not reading my mind. He's grieving and has little interest in learning his mage powers. His attitude is not about me. Really. It's not.

I hope.

I rub a shaky hand against my forehead, draw in a deep breath, and release it hard. The prospect of introspection instead of a mental prep for a busy evening fails to put me in my happy place. Knowing Will wants to avoid me since I represent Smythe and the Agency churns an ache in my chest.

Leaning against the cool metal of the lockers, I close my eyes and shove all my baggage deep inside for review on my way home. Right now my mind needs to be in the game, ready for a hard night's work, not circling around like a shark hungry for a meal.

When my eyes open, I'm in the present, ready to go, mind on the patients.

Chapter Seven

I no sooner step into my kitchen than Smythe storms out of the living room, eyes lit with a glee normally seen in misbehaving puppies. Never a good sign after a long evening at work.

"You're late."

He should know by now my shift might technically end at eleven, but chances are good I won't be leaving until midnight. The clock reads 12:15, the click-click of the minute hand a reminder I need to sit and relax.

"Yeah. That's what happens in the ER." I set my purse on the counter and pull a glass out of the cabinet.

"You look tired."

My mentor, master of the obvious.

"Again." I point the empty glass at him. "That's what happens in the ER."

"You can't back out tonight. Your outfit is on the bed. Hurry up and change."

I blink several times, as if that will cause his words to have different meanings. "Come again? Change? What outfit are you talking about?" What in my closet did he pull out?

"The police talked to Jenny's friends." He grabs the glass out of my slack hand, setting it on the counter. "They hung out together at Club Monster before she left with Donny. They didn't see her after that. We need to go to the club."

"Seriously? It's after midnight."

He shrugs. "It's a club. Hurry up."

"I just got home from work." I grab the glass and shove it into the water dispenser on the fridge.

"It's Friday night." His words wrap around me, a hint of irritation in the undertones. I shiver, shove my stupid learned reaction to fear aside, and turn to face him.

"No. I'm exhausted." What does he expect? Me to be all happy about going back out after a long evening?

He stares at me for a long pause. "I'm sorry. But we need to go to the club and see if we can get a lead on the minion who killed Jenny. Before they strike again."

Good point. Although, an unfortunate one for my tired self. I suppose I can suck it up for Smythe. An exhausted demon-huntress is better than none at all.

So much for relaxing at the end of a long evening.

"Fine." I give him a glare guaranteed to make a cantankerous patient straighten up and fly right as I swallow the water in one long gulp. Smythe's eyes narrow. At least he doesn't seem mad. More like excited to track a minion.

An emotion the ER sucked right out of me.

An emotion I need to get back. After all, I don't wear the *justitia* for nothing. Might as well use the bracelet for something other than a pretty bauble.

"What did you pick out for me? I'm pretty sure all my clubbing outfits are long gone." Too many people packed together in one too-small place for my liking. Too many opportunities to touch, and most clubbers don't have candy canes and rainbows on their mind.

I never thought I'd hear myself say this, but I'm

too old for that shit.

The pleased glint in his gaze morphs into worry. "I went shopping."

Oh now, this I've got to see. Keeping my thoughts to myself, I raise a brow as a response and walk into my room. A quick flick of the light switch brings my outfit into view.

Shiny blue material forms a barely there, skin-tight dress sprawled on my bed. At least it sports long sleeves. Blue heels sit on the floor waiting for my feet. I'm about to protest the heels when I notice their tell-tale red soles. Oh my god, he bought me an uber-expensive pair of shoes I could never afford on a good day. Yeah, I can cram my achy feet into those pointy-toed beasts if only to say I am wearing a pair of outrageously expensive shoes.

"You like?"

I start at his voice right behind me. *Gah*, I need to pay more attention to my surroundings. A heart attack is not on my to-do list for the day.

"You bought me expensive shoes." I point at them, as if there's any doubt which pair.

"The dress is designer too." A hint of uncertainty flows through his tone.

I look at the tag and blink several times. Yep, designer. Yep, expensive. "I can't afford these."

He shrugs as he stares at the dress. "Club Monster is a fancy club. You'll fit in better in expensive clothes. And you didn't pay for them. These are for work. Consider it a one-time perk."

I look at the dress, then at Smythe, then back at the dress. Stupid moisture pools in my eyes causing me to blink fast in order to see straight. I've never owned such nice clothes in my life. Damn straight I can wear the outfit. "Okay." I clear my throat. "A perk it is. What are you wearing?"

"Clothes." A grin turns one side of his lips.

I shake my head. "Never would've guessed."

"My role tonight isn't as important as yours. You need to bait Donny. See if you can get him to say where Jenny went after their bathroom escapade."

"He never said they had one. I saw it in his thoughts."

"Yep. And now you need to get him to admit it. Maybe he saw someone else following her."

"Maybe he didn't."

Brows furrow as his gaze grows distant with thought. "There's something off about this situation."

"Yeah. She was killed by a minion."

"Besides the obvious."

"Like what?" *The strange way the minion trails coalesced around Donny last night before dissipating?*

"Is it a coincidence Jenny was killed after she met with Donny?"

"I thought we already established he wasn't a minion and therefore not the killer."

"He could have killed her, then hired a minion to dispose of the body. Maybe that was why he was so surprised to see her. He didn't expect the minion to dispose of the body at the stadium."

"Or he's innocent." I refuse to believe Donny killed Jenny. Dumped her, yeah. Banged one of her friends, sure. But kill her? Nah. He didn't seem the type.

"Either way, you need to get a move on. It's not going to take you long to dress, is it?"

"Shoo." I wave my hands toward the door, and he obliges, pulling the door closed behind him.

In no time at all, my scrubs are in the laundry basket, and I'm taking a speedy shower. After drying off, I pull on a clean bra and panties, then slide the blue dress over my head. The smooth feel of the material rubs against my skin in a way that screams expensive. I twist my hair into a bun and apply enough mascara and eye shadow to make my lids heavy. A dose of lipstick later and I look at myself in the mirror.

The dress hugs my hips, hangs two hands past my girlie parts and displays cleavage like a high-priced hooker. The red-soled shoes pinch my toes, but I refuse to complain. The things I do in the line of duty.

When I open my bedroom door, Smythe leans against the wall, arms crossed, wearing black trousers, a white button-down shirt, and a black jacket.

"Why, Smythe, you have clothes that aren't black jeans and t-shirts."

Instead of shooting me a get-real stare, his hooded gaze rakes my body from head to toe and back, leaving my core prickly and eager. Memories of our shared kiss swim through my mind, a remembrance I don't need to touch him to know he sees too. Visions stream into possibilities as the scent of desire fills the air.

But being a *Justitian* comes before bedding the boss.

Damn it.

I clear my throat and hold out my arms, knowing the answer even as I ask the question. "Whatcha think?"

"You look…nice." Deep tones saturate a voice heavy with need.

I smooth the front of the dress. "You did a good

job with the sizes."

"Thanks." One side of his mouth kicks up. A long pause and he holds out his arm. "Ready?"

Hard muscles under my fingers contrast with the smoothness of his jacket. He holds out a hand and speaks his portal-forming words. We land in an alley, a block away from Club Monster.

The deep throb of distant bass punctuates our silence, broken only by our shoes hitting the concrete. We are almost to the end of the line—yes, at 12:45 a.m. there is still a line to enter—when Smythe speaks.

"We'll split once we get inside. Look for minions, but don't engage. We need to obtain information on the killer."

Like I can engage a minion in a skin-tight dress and too-tight heels without pulling the skirt up around my waist and kicking off the shoes. I'm not seeing jail time for indecent exposure in my future. "It's not Donny."

"If you see him, try to get information."

"I know." I swallow the irritation in my tone. "We've done this before."

"Not like this we haven't."

Okay, good point. "How are we getting in?"

"Leave it to me."

We bypass the line, ignore the yells and a few whistles, and walk right up to the guard checking IDs. He points to the end of the line, but Smythe whispers something I don't catch and snaps his fingers, and the guard's gaze fuzzes as he falls under the spell. So much for paying the entry fee.

Doors open for us as the guard speaks into a mic on his wrist. Deep bass thrums a rhythm in my chest, my bones vibrating to its welcoming beat. Cold air blows a greeting as we walk inside. Lights sparkle from the ceiling, forming pink and purple puddles on the floor. Smoke hovers like a miasma as bodies press together on the dance floor, too many to count, all writhing with need. Smythe heads toward the bar, me following in his wake, trying not to touch anyone.

Wishful thinking. At least the long sleeves offer protection from others' emotions.

Halfway to the bar, a tingle zips across my nerves, the *justitia* shaking with awareness. Demon? Or minion? Confusion follows as my bracelet attempts to locate the source and comes up negative. I glance around the club, my gaze skimming across the writhing dancers, before rising to the second story. A balcony overlooks the dance floor, patrons leaning against the metal railing. One man rests palms against the railing, overlooking the dancers. I stop, my breath frozen in my lungs. Time slows as the man's gaze sweeps my direction. Dark hair frames a face hidden in shadows. In the dim light, it's hard to see his expression, yet the prickles exploding across my skin leave no doubt about the object of his stare.

Me.

Unlike the stares men give an attractive woman, his attention washes over me, leaving behind a strange sensation. I stand straighter, shoulders back, chin up, as if imagining myself successful. Which I am. Or I wouldn't be a kickass demon huntress.

He slides from the shadows, enough for me to see his lower face. A smile turns his full lips into a parody of a grin as he continues to stare at me. As if he wants to drink me dry.

The man nods, turns, and disappears into the crowd.

Could he be the reason my *justitia* senses a demon presence? Or was he just some creepy stranger out for a good time?

Only one way to find out: an up-close and personal meeting.

Someone grabs my elbow. An embarrassing squeak passes my lips. My heart beats double time. Was it the man from the balcony? No way. A human couldn't move that fast. And since my *justitia* remained in bracelet form, clearly it wasn't a minion or demon.

Annoying human, then.

I turn to my accoster, get-back glare at the ready, only to stare agape at the obvious bodyguard. No one comes in that size unless they are packing heat. The huge-ass man leans forward, his voice pitched so low I barely hear him over the pounding bass.

"Donny would like to see you."

I blink in surprise. So much for needing to search the place for Donny. Not that I'm complaining. Mr. Oversized Bodyguard just saved me some time.

I glance to the balcony, but the man remains absent. I'll hunt for him after I see Donny. Taking a deep breath, I nod at the bodyguard.

"Okay. Where's he at?"

The bodyguard leads me through the club to a private room. Oo-la-la. Two steps from the room and Smythe pops into my head.

Gin? Where are you?

About to talk with Donny. I need to go.

Okay. Good.

And he's gone. Good thing too. I need all my

brainpower to interrogate Donny without him realizing what I'm doing.

Donny smiles at me from where he sits on an overstuffed red sofa surrounded by fellow football players and several women. Most of the men's gazes rake my body like I'm a new food dish, while the women shoot me go-to-hell glances.

Talk about uncomfortable.

I draw in a breath, paste on a smile, and put a swing to my hips as I saunter to Donny.

"Hey. You wanted to see me?"

"Yeah, baby." He gestures to me, and the guy sitting next to him scoots over, giving me a foot of space to squeeze in next to the football star.

I sit, my legs pressing against Donny and the guy to my left. At least they wear pants, and my long sleeves protect against wayward emotions and thoughts. Nice of Smythe to think of my touch-and-see problem when he bought me this dress.

"Want a drink?"

Just what I need. I lick my lips, imagining the taste of whiskey caressing my tongue, warming my stomach. I've been good since my younger years, keeping myself to beer in small doses, once I realized a nursing degree was my key to pulling myself up by my bootstraps. I've been so good; I know I can handle a fancy drink. Just one. Just to fit in. No problem.

"Sure." I swallow away a niggling sense of guilt. "Whatcha drinking?"

"Tequila. Whiskey. But they"—he points at the nearest woman snuggled next to one of his friends—"are drinking, what is that?"

"A Cosmo." The woman smiles, all teeth and

jealousy.

"Yeah. One of those. Want one of those?"

"I'm not a fruity concoction type of gal." I straighten my shoulders, drawing in a deep breath. "I'll take a whiskey. Neat."

He nods, approval in his eyes. When he raises a hand a server steps up like she'd been hiding in the corner waiting for his signal. He gives her our drink orders and waves her off.

"What brings you to Club Monster, babe?"

"Just wanted some fun." I shrug. "You come here often?"

"Looking to find me?" A grin plays across his face as one brow rises.

Heat slaps my cheeks. "I'm here, aren't I?"

Gah, Gin, dial it back. Who knew being an investigator was so hard?

"You found me. Now you know my place."

"Your place?"

"This"—he opens his arms to encompass the room—"this is my place, you know? Football, home, and here."

"And the charity." I smile, offering him a wink.

"Charities." Donny draws out the *s*, a grin curving his lips.

He wraps one arm around my shoulders, while he puts his other hand on my knee, thumb stroking the inner skin of my thigh. A shot of lust zips from his thumb straight to my core. His lust, not mine. Right when the emotion morphs into his imagining us naked, I shift, hoping to dislodge his hand without looking obvious.

Yeah, he's hot, and I could easily fall for his

charms. But he could also be a killer, and I'm supposed to be solving a crime, not getting it on with the football star. As sad as it sounds, I'm holding out for a six-foot-five hunk with blue eyes and dark hair.

Gah.

Head in the game, Gin. Head in the game.

Steeling myself, I place my hand over his and scoot his hand back onto his knee. Giving him a wink, I pat his hand, while ignoring his lustful irritation pinging through my veins.

"Now, now."

He raises both hands. "You can't blame a guy for trying."

"I suppose not." I offer him a grin.

"This your first time here?"

"How'd you know?"

"My place, remember?"

"Speaking of, how'd you know I was here?" I point to the door. "It's not like you can see out there."

One corner of his mouth kicks up. "Trade secret."

"Right. Your place."

He chuckles, takes our drinks from the server and hands me mine. "You got it."

I glance at the amber liquid in my glass while the server flits to the guy sitting next to me. A thin bead of sweat slips down my spine.

"You gonna drink that or stare at it all night?" Donny smiles and clinks my glass.

I draw in a deep breath, offer him a half grin and take a sip. The whiskey slides down my throat and hits my stomach with a rush of heat and pleasure. Ten years have passed since I had a sip of the hard stuff. Ten long years. I've been good. And I'll be good tonight. It's just one drink.

I take another sip. "Thanks for the drink."

"Anything for a pretty lady."

"Aw, Donny, I bet you say that to all the ladies."

"Not tonight."

"I'm honored. But..." I let the words trail into silence as I sip my drink, staring at him over the rim of the glass.

"I know. You walked in with him."

"Him?" He saw me with Smythe?

"The bigass FBI guy."

Damn. He did see me with Smythe. "You know?"

"My place, remember?"

"Sorry." Not even five minutes in and my cover is already blown.

"Nothing to be sorry for. Didn't realize FBI agents could drink on the job."

"I'm not an agent." I raise my glass and down the whiskey, loving the burn. A few more of these and I won't have to worry about the long sleeves, the alcohol will kill the empathic ability.

Without needing a gesture, the server appears with another round of drinks. I don't need the second one, but expensive whiskey shouldn't be wasted.

"Not an agent, eh. Then why are you here with one?"

So much for stealth. The truth feels foreign on my tongue. "We were hoping to catch a killer."

He raises a brow, then takes a sip of his drink to hide the grin spreading across his lips. "What can I do to help?"

"Tell me what happened after you left Jenny."

He settles back into the sofa, glass resting on his

leg. A quick gesture to the bodyguard ends seconds later with a cleared room, leaving us alone with the guard and serving crew. Perfect for an in-depth interrogation.

"She was fine when I left her." His gaze drops to his glass as he takes a sip. "I came back here and didn't see where she went. I assumed she went back with her friends, but clearly that didn't happen."

Did he leave her in the bathroom? Or did she leave him? Since he doesn't offer that little tidbit of TMI, and to tell him I knew would give away my super-secret empath ability, I move on to the next obvious question. "Who were her friends?"

"Don't know. I mean, I'd never seen them before. I just met her that night. We danced, came back here, went to…dance again, then I came back here. Didn't see her after that. Until, well, you know."

"Yeah." I take a long swallow of the whiskey. "Did you notice anything out of place that night?"

"No." He starts to shake his head, then narrows his eyes. "Wait. There was this guy, called me by name. 'Hey-ya, Donny.' Like he knew me or something."

Somebody tried to meet Donny. Like that never happens. But one look at the serious expression on his face stops my smartass remark. The fact this guy named him really bothers Donny. I offer him a grin, aiming, instead, for sympathetic. "You're famous around here."

"I guess. But he was different from the typical fan. I'm telling you, he acted like he knew me."

I suppose being a celebrity means Donny possesses a finely tuned creep sense. Either that or he's paranoid.

"How so?"

He shrugs. "The way he looked at me. How he

tried to talk like we were friends or something. You could tell he was all jealous of Jenny. Like he belonged to me, you know? Weird."

"Yeah, that is weird." In more ways than one. "What did he look like?"

"Normal. White guy. Brown hair, brown eyes. Nothing out of place. Come to think of it, he did look familiar. Like maybe I knew him. From long ago. I meet a lot of people." He shrugs, taking a sip of his drink.

I debate whether or not to touch him in hopes of seeing the man. But only for a second. Intruding into the bathroom scene last night makes me wary of another trip into Donny's head. Best to file away the man's description for Smythe's internet hacking skills.

"Weird." Maybe he met the guy at a charity event. Would explain the guy acting like he knew Donny and Donny's lack of remembrance.

"Yeah. Definitely." He upends his drink. "Wanna dance?"

Hoping "dance" isn't a euphemism for extracurricular bathroom activities, I swallow my drink, almost purring in ecstasy as the burn settles in my stomach. A tendril of guilt wends through my mind, but I squash it. Two drinks does not a relapse make. Placing my hand on his sleeved arm, I allow him to pull me to my feet.

And then the server plops two more drinks on our table. Geez Louise, how much does she make to be johnny-on-the-spot like that? Probably a lot.

I grab my drink, unwilling to let it sit by itself. No telling what might be in it when I return.

"Leave it."

I look at the drink, then Donny. "Donny, Donny, Donny, don'tcha know a girl shouldn't leave a drink sitting alone? No telling who might put what in it."

"That won't—" His words die on his tongue as I swallow half the drink in one fluid gulp and lightly shake the remainder before my face.

"No, it won't. I'm taking it with me."

Donny laughs. "I like you. Come on, let's dance."

This time when he grabs my hand, no annoying thoughts or emotions ping my mind. Mission accomplished. Thanks, whiskey.

We no sooner leave the room than a medium-sized guy with a bad dye job runs into us. More like runs into me. My drink sloshes over the rim onto my hand and part of my sleeve. Great. Now my new designer dress is going to smell like a brewery.

"Sorry," he mutters, staggering out of the way.

"You okay?" Donny glares at the guy's back before turning to me. For a second, I think he's going to chase after the guy, instead he grips my hand hard enough for the bones to move.

I flinch, and he drops my hand.

"Sorry."

"I'm tough." Tougher than he'll ever know.

"You might as well put down the glass. It's almost empty."

A glance proves him right. What a waste of fine whiskey.

I swallow the remaining few sips and place the glass on a conveniently located ledge that served well as a depository for empty glasses. My stomach lurches in protest of not enough food and too much liquor. A zip of electricity darts through my veins, courtesy of the *justitia.*

Strange. Maybe the loud music bothers the entity in the bracelet?

By the time we arrive at the dance floor, the room spins with lights. Or maybe the lights spin the room. Either way a remote possibility exists that I shouldn't have thrown back two and a half whiskeys faster than a dehydrated man drinks from an oasis. But it's just once in ten years.

Not bad. I'm still doing okay. I'm still in charge.

I trip on the dance floor, falling onto Donny. "Oops. It's the heels." Whiskey has nothing to do with my ability, or lack thereof, to walk.

He catches me one handed. Guess he's used to one-handed catches. I chuckle.

"What?"

"You caught me one-handed. Like I'm a ball." My words slur. They shouldn't. Should they?

Donny shakes his head. Either he didn't hear me over the music or was too put-off by my comment to answer.

Time slides by, spinning the room with it, until I'm no longer sure if dancing is such a great idea. Maybe I should leave. After all, I learned what I came here for.

I think. I'm no longer sure.

"I'm gonna go." I shout close to Donny's ear to make sure he hears me over the music.

He jerks. Maybe I yelled a bit too loud.

"Do you have to go?" He leans close, the liquor on his breath caressing my skin.

I pull back. "It might be best."

"Whiskey caught up with you?"

"Don't be silly."

His expression indicates he sees through my lie. But he escorts me off the dance floor like a gentleman, one hand against my lower back.

"Will you come back?"

"Here?"

"Where else?"

"You want me to?"

He shrugs. "You interest me."

"Why, Donny…" I slap a hand against his chest, pull it away in embarrassment. "That'shuch a nice thing to shay to a girl."

His laughter coats me in good times. "Friends?"

"Shure, Donny. Friends. Shee you around?"

"The FBI dude taking you home, or should I call you a cab?"

"He'sh takin' me home." I hope. Smythe is here, right? Wherever here might be. I should know the answer to that question. Donny looks at me, one brow raised. Right. He asked me something I didn't hear. I giggle. "Thanksh. Had fun. Thankss for the whish, whish, um, the drinksh." *Gah*, what was wrong with me?

"You sure you're fine?"

I nod. Bad idea. The room swirls a nasty jig.

"See ya 'round, then." And with those words, he disappears into the crowd.

The music pulses in my chest, the deep beat thumping in time with my heart. *Smythe?*

Gin? Are you okay?

I don't know.

Where are you?

Here.

"Ma'am? Are you okay?" A familiar-looking guy

with a bad dye job grabs my arm. Good thing too, my legs wobble like a newborn calf.

I nod as he leads me away from the noise. Where's Smythe? Weren't we talking? A dull buzz takes up residence in my mind, obliterating any chance of telepathic conversation. My vision focuses on the man holding my arm as the club patrons fade into background noise.

He pushes open a door to a long hall. The door snaps shut behind us, an echo of finality. A ball of writhing snakes forms in my stomach. The thudding pulse of music lessens, replaced by the clip of our shoes against concrete as we head toward the end. Dim lights shine from recessed bulbs. I blink. The light hurts.

"We shhhhhhouldn't be back here."

"Nonsense. I'm going to help you." He drags me down the hall, my legs refusing to resist.

A deep *thump-thump* thrashes in my ears, blood pumping a racing rhythm through tense veins. I shouldn't be here. I need to leave.

But I can't remember how.

The hall narrows to a small tunnel filled with dancing black spots as my legs wobble, unable to hold weight. Pain bruises my knees, my shoulder aches as the guy tightens his hold. My stomach roils, emptying its meager contents on the dark concrete floor.

"Damn it. You're supposed to pass out, not throw up."

What does he mean?

Under half-closed lids, I peer up his arm, over his clenched jaw, into his narrowed eyes. The light makes me blink. Pain spreads from his grip on my arm, nerve endings firing in protest. His outline blurs as my eyes water. Black spots dart around the periphery of my vision.

That means something. Something not good.

The man yanks, tearing the skin off my knees as he pulls me along the ground. At least he avoided the puddle of puke. I struggle to get my feet under me. I need to be upright.

But nothing works.

My knees refuse to hold my weight. My arm hangs limp and throbbing in his grasp. My other arm should hit him, should try to break free but, instead, drags along the ground like an arthritic monkey, in a vain attempt to keep my body upright. Black spots creep across my vision, a silent plea to close my eyes, to end this suffering.

I don't want to close my eyes. Bad things happen when my eyes close.

I try to open them wider, but my lids are heavy. So, so heavy.

Help! Help me! My mind cries the words, my lips unable to move.

And then my eyes close. My hearing fades until I'm muffled in the soundlessness of darkness.

Hold on, Gin! I'm coming!

Smythe's voice screams through my mind, the bellow of a bear protecting its mate. But not even knowing he comes can rouse me. Hearing gone, I slip into unconsciousness, the scent of blood mingled with puke following me into the blackness.

Chapter Eight

I wake to the warm comfort of softness against my back. Voices hum in the background, pleasing, comforting. I nestle deeper into the warmth. I am safe.

Why that thought?

And then I remember, my mind tripping backward in time. Where was I?

I shoot upright as if propelled by an invisible hand. "Wh—"

The Agency healer, Eloise, and Smythe stand by the door to my bedroom. I'm lying on the bed still wearing my designer dress, my shoeless feet on the pillows, my head where my feet should rest. Nothing hurts, and my vision is clear and spotless.

I clear my throat. "What happened?"

"I should ask the same of you." Smythe raises a brow.

I swing my legs over the edge of the bed and rub the bridge of my nose. "Thank you for the healing, Eloise." Despite my lack of memory of her healing, I'm certain she didn't show up to watch me sleep.

"You are welcome." The melodious lilt of her voice turns my lips into a smile.

"T's not here."

A tinge of color flashes across her pale cheeks. "Did I ask for him?"

You didn't have to sits on my tongue, erased by

Smythe's interruption.

"You are our topic of discussion, not your brother." He moves to stand in front of me, arms crossed. "What the hell happened? You smelled like whiskey, and Eloise said you'd been drugged."

Relief courses through me. Drugged, not drunk. Even after ten years I can handle a couple of drinks. *Wait*. Drugged? Anger sucker punches the relief out of my system.

"Drugged? Someone drugged me? Who would do that?"

Of course, Donny hops to the top of the list. I don't need to read Smythe's mind to see he reached the same conclusion. Donny might be on the top of the list, but I still don't think he did it. Okay, maybe I just don't want him to be guilty. He's the Generous Charity-Giver, the all-around nice guy. However, he did call the club "his place." The VIP server was speedy to hand us our drinks. Could he have arranged to have the server put something into my drink? How would he have known I was coming to the club?

I'm not actually thinking Donny, Mr. Charity Donator and football star extraordinaire, drugged my drink, am I?

At this point, I'm clinging to his innocence with my fingernails.

"Donny's a lot of things, but a drugger of women's drinks is not one of them."

"Are you sure about that?"

My mouth opens. Shuts. Opens again. Before I can get the words out, Smythe nods.

"You aren't sure about that. He could've killed Jenny and hired a minion to dispose of her body."

"I don't think so." I shake my head. "He doesn't seem like the killer type."

"Neither did Jeffrey Dahmer."

"It's not the same thing."

Smythe shoots me a get-real look. I ignore it.

"He said he left Jenny and returned to his room. Did you know he has his own private room at Club Monster?"

"Killers say whatever to get off the hook."

"I don't think he killed her. He definitely didn't tinker with my drinks."

"Drinks?" Smythe's jaw tightens.

I flinch. Silly, damn ingrained reaction. To cover, I shrug. "I had to fit in, right? Get him to confide in me. It worked, by the way. He said he liked me, and I should come back and visit him. That proves he didn't drug my drink. Why would he ask me back if he did?"

"Why wouldn't he?" Smythe rubs his forehead. "Never mind. If you don't think he drugged your drink, then how do you explain how you were drugged?"

"I don't know. How did you find me? What happened to the guy dragging me?"

"Dragging you?" The expression on Smythe's face morphs from curious to murderous in under a second. His fingers flex. At least his anger isn't directed at me this time. Part of me feels sorry for the guy with the bad dye job.

It's a small part and easily squashed.

"I was dancing with Donny and started feeling sick. Like I was drunk but a hundred times worse. He asked if he should call me a cab, I think, then he left and Bad Dye Job showed up."

"Who?"

"This guy had a horrid blond dye job." A memory of leaving Donny's room jerks my eyes wide. "He ran into me. When Donny and I left his room. Donny's room. For the dance floor. We walked into the main club, and that guy ran into me. Hit me hard enough to splash my drink all over my sleeve. It was after that I started feeling sick. He must've drugged me, not Donny."

"Donny could've hired him." Smythe stalks the few steps to where Eloise stands, his fingers flexing open, closed, open, closed. "You haven't explained the dragging. What do you mean, the guy dragged you?"

"Right. Sorry. After Donny left, I ran into the bad dye job guy. Again. I can't really remember what happened, but he led me to through doors to a hallway. Maybe in the back of the club? Or where the offices were? I don't know, but I couldn't walk. I threw up. Then he started dragging me. I couldn't stand, and my knees got all scratched."

I peer at my knees, happy to note no scratches, tears, or marks. Eloise's healing rocks.

My gaze meets Smythe's enraged one. At least all that anger focuses on some target other than me.

"How did you find me?" My voice lands one note up from a whisper.

"Followed your cry for help to that hall by the club offices. You were on the floor, and some guy was bending over you. I asked what he was doing with my friend, and he said he was trying to put you in the office to sleep it off since you were so wasted. He took off down the hall and out the doors into the club when I bent to see about you. I fuzzed the cameras and portaled you home." He smacks a palm against the wall. "I shouldn't have believed him."

Eloise pats his arm, her blind stare focused on me. "You need to be taught how to tell when your drink is poisoned."

"It was drugged, not poisoned."

She waves a hand, negating my correction. "Same difference."

Not really, but I'm not in the mood to argue. "Why didn't the *justitia* nullify the effects? Like it does when it helps me heal faster?"

"*Justitias* don't work against poison. Which is why you need to learn to detect it."

Nice to know. Better late than never, I suppose.

"How do I learn to taste a tasteless substance?"

"You don't taste it. You detect it with a spell before it passes your lips."

"I didn't think spells were in a *Justitian's* bag of tricks."

"They aren't." Smythe narrows his eyes, silently glaring Eloise into silence.

It fails.

"Nonsense." Eloise waves away his words. "Anyone can be taught a detection spell."

"Eloise." Smythe lowers his voice, enunciating each word as if explaining physics to kindergarteners. "Mages perform spells. *Justitians* kill demons. Not the other way around."

Only a *justitia* can kill a demon. Mages help us with their spells, but no spell can take down one of Hell's own.

"She can be taught."

"By who?" Smythe gives Eloise a puzzled glance. "I don't know that type of spell."

Well, I learned something new. I thought Smythe knew every spell. Shows you what I know. Or don't know as the case may be.

"Perhaps a lesson for all is in order. Tomorrow evening? Here?" Eloise turns to me. "Be sure to invite your brother." And with those final words, she forms a portal and disappears. Nifty trick to avoid disagreement.

The look Smythe shoots at the closing portal is as cold as the portal itself. He drums long fingers against his thigh.

"I'm assuming she means to talk to T about becoming a ghost talker."

Only if talking is an euphemism for getting it on with my twin. Can't Smythe see what's going on between the two of them?

"Assume all you want. You know what they say about it." My grin fades as memories of the club swamp my mind. Breath catches in lungs tight with emotion. "Thank you for rescuing me. I don't know what would've happened if you hadn't come along."

He steps closer to me, his palm warm upon my shoulder.

"I shouldn't have put you in a position to get hurt."

"Smythe. You put me in those types of positions on a daily basis and call it my job."

He removes his palm, sitting next to me as he speaks.

"That's different. You know what I mean."

I suppose I do. Although rattling his cage is half the fun. "Yeah. I guess I do." Fighting the walking evil goes with the job. Being drugged at a club by a potential killer is a whole different issue. "I don't know why they tried to drug me."

"They didn't try. They succeeded."

"Semantics." I wave a hand. "Why me?"

"No clue. It could have something to do with Jenny. It might not. Donny might have tried to scare you off."

"He could've just said leave instead of inviting me back for a drink. No, I disagree with you about him. He's not a killer. Or a man who feels the need to drug women's drinks."

"If you say so."

"I do. Enough about Donny. I want to find that guy who drugged my drink. I didn't even meet him. What about me made him choose me?"

"As I said, I don't know." Smythe punctuates his words with a shrug and head shake. "But I'll get online and see if I can find the cameras for the club. Are you okay?"

"Thanks to you. I'm glad you're always around to save my ass since I've become a demon huntress. I don't know what I'd do without you." Probably be dead. A chill snakes down my spine, and I cover it with a half smile.

"That's what I'm here for. And it's *Justitian*, not demon huntress." He returns my grin, his gaze dropping to my lips as red creeps high on his cheeks. He pops off the bed faster than a cork freed from a champagne bottle. One palm pats my shoulder twice, a failed attempt at eradicating the strings of potential passion spreading between us. "I'll be in the other room. Try to get some sleep. It's late. Or early."

"Yeah. Thanks." Sleep is the last thing on my mind, tiredness banished by Eloise's healing.

Smythe stares at me, narrowed eyes seeing into my soul. What does he see inside me? Invisible ribbons band us together, pulling him into me, me into him, a tie we continue to ignore.

He clears his throat, the moment evaporating. "See you tomorrow. I mean, later today."

The door snaps closed behind him, tension deflating from the room. Red numbers glow 4:00 a.m. on the alarm clock, a reminder to become exhausted. And yet, I'm pumped, running on adrenaline, leftover healing energy, and sexual frustration, the mix a buzz of impatience trapped beneath my skin.

I need sleep, which means I need out of this dress.

A quick dash into the bathroom followed by a change of clothes along with a make-up removal session and I'm ready for bed. As soon as I walk into my bedroom I draw in a breath, thoughts of sleep vanquished by a rush of intimidation mixed with longing.

Zagan leans against the wall on the other side of my bed, arms crossed, biceps straining against the fabric of his white button-down shirt. The demon of deceit. The demon who mistakenly believes I am his servant. The demon my *justitia* sees as a friend.

Traitorous jumping-for-joy bracelet.

I shake my wrist, as if that will stop the silver links from clicking together with joy.

"Zagan. What are you doing in my bedroom?"

"I find I like it here." A smile turns his lips as his gaze drifts across my face. "So homey."

"I smell a lie."

He shrugs. "I am the demon of deceit, am I not?"

"Out with it." I circle my hand, encouraging him to

talk.

"I wanted to see how you were doing." He pushes off the wall, taking a step toward me, the tone of his voice a mesmerizing pull. "Is that so wrong? Do not friends talk to each other?"

I stop short of telling him he's not my friend. He's my *justitia's* friend. The only demon my bracelet refuses to kill. Refuses to let me kill.

Oh, who am I trying to fool? Whether due to the entity in the bracelet attached to my nervous system or personal preference, during the time I've worn the *justitia*, Zagan has become somewhat of a friend.

In the loosest definition of the word.

Not that I'd tell him. Wouldn't want him to get any more ideas than he already has. And trust me, he's been full of ideas since the first time we met.

At least he can't force me to obey him.

Which makes me an enigma to the demon. An enigma I can handle. Obeying him, not so much.

"What do you want to discuss?"

"You were injured tonight."

"Damn. News travels fast." Really freaking fast if he already knew.

"I am a demon who listens." He stalks a step closer, eyes narrowing. "Why were you at the club?"

"I thought you said you listened."

He waves a hand. "I did not hear that part of the story. Do tell."

What harm could there be? Maybe Zagan will offer the name of Jenny's killer. Since the damn demon knows the murderer's identity.

"Jenny, the woman whose body was found at the Armadillos' stadium the other night, was last seen at

Club Monster. We were trying to find the minion who killed her."

"Ah. And did you?"

"No. But someone drugged me. And tried to drag me off the premises." I shudder and shove the memory aside. I will not think of how close I came to something bad in Zagan's presence.

He snarls, fingers cranking into fists. "You should not be harmed."

I can't stop the eye roll. "What is it with you guys? Smythe said almost the same thing. Come on. I'm a freaking *Justitian.* I kill minions and demons, present company excluded. It's not like I don't get hurt regularly." Despite my no-big-deal talk, my hands tremble, a delayed adrenaline rush from my near-death experience.

Not that I'll tell Zagan. Better he think I'm a strong independent woman instead of a scared little girl putting on a brave face.

His snarl relaxes, but the air vibrates around him, a distant storm on the horizon.

"That is different. You cannot use a *justitia* against a human."

I drop my gaze, focusing on stilling the trembling shaking my limbs. "Yeah. I found that out the hard way. Don't worry, it won't happen again." No more whiskey for me.

Zagan steps closer, his voice a low growl bent on revenge. "You are correct. It will not happen again. I will find the one who dared to poison your drink. I will—"

My gaze snaps up to meet his murderous glare. I hold up a hand. "Whoa, buddy. I so do not want to hear any murder plans. That makes me a witness in a court of law. No planning to kill humans around me. You hear?"

Zagan blinks, rant ending as a grin spreads his lips wide. "You called me buddy. We truly are friends."

After my don't-talk-to-me-about-murdering-humans speech, *that's* all he has to say? Not an "okay" or "no way," just a comment on how my poor word choice indicates a friendship?

Demons. You never know how they might twist your words to suit their purposes.

Although, being Zagan's friend beats the alternative of being his servant. Truth be told, I like the idea of having this particular demon for a friend.

Gah. Where's a convenient brain transplant surgeon when I need one? This emotional state of conflict is driving me crazy.

"Why is being my friend so important to you?"

"You wound me." He places a hand over his heart in mock horror. "Can a demon not enjoy a human's companionship? Her witty humor? The way her heart beats for me?"

"Don't delude yourself on that last point. Buddy."

One side of his mouth kicks up, and he takes a step toward me. "We have been through this before. Your blood calls to me. I answer."

"You answer because you and my *justitia* have history together. It has nothing to do with me." I swallow, acting all tough-girl while my insides twist into quivering ropes.

"That is where you are wrong, Gin." I suck down a breath as he steps in front of me, as he places his hand over my heart. "You called to me before"—the name of my *justitia* rolls off his tongue, a name unpronounceable on human lips—"became part of you. Long before. One day you will realize how much I helped you and be grateful." The last word he whispers in my ear, leaving a trail of chills to dance across my skin.

Spit dries in my mouth. Does he mean what I fear he does? Had he been attracted to me because of the lies I told my entire life? Could my ultimate deception be what called him to me?

Was it possible his attraction had nothing to do with my *justitia?*

When he steps out of my personal space, I shiver with relief. Time for a topic change, STAT.

"Why was Jenny killed?"

"You might believe her death to be tragic, but you need to focus on the more pressing issue."

"What's more pressing than a rampaging minion killing women?"

"A rampaging demon ensnaring humans to do its bidding."

"There's a demon loose on earth?" So much for the Agency demon-appearance computer program working.

"Not loose. Ensnaring. Thinking it's better than all the rest. That it should be the leader of all forces in Hell." His fingers flex and release as a snarl forms only to fade. He pierces me with a direct gaze. "It will use humans to do its bidding. You need to stop this demon."

"Geez, Zagan. That sounds like every other demon, including you, out there." Despite my bravo, a sense of foreboding brushes a finger down my spine. I straighten.

"This demon is not me. I am wounded you think it is." He places a hand over his heart, while pouting like I hurt his feelings.

Which I'm pretty sure is an act.

"Okay, I'll bite. How do I stop it?"

"Find the one the demon targets." He drops that bomb as if there's only one person targeted by a demon in the whole United States.

Seriously? "Which one?"

"The one the demon wants." He enunciates each word as if I'm slow and don't understand the language. "But be careful. If you are harmed again—"

I hold up my hand. "Nuh-uh. Remember? No murder plans or threats to humans in front of me."

He pauses. Blinks twice. A ghost of a smile plays across his lips.

"As you wish. You know what I will do to them without me needing to say it."

I shiver. I do know. I almost feel sorry for the poor bastard. Almost.

"I am glad you are well." His gaze rakes my body, clinical, not sexual, yet chills blossom on my flesh.

"Thank you." I clear my throat to bring my voice down an octave. "And thank Eloise."

"Ah." His eyes sparkle with an inhuman fire at the mention of the healer's name. "Eloise. It has been many years since I have seen her. You are in good hands. I will leave you now." He circles one hand, palm up to form a portal.

"Wait!"

But he doesn't, disappearing into his portal before I can ask how he knows the Agency healer. Damn it. Yet another mystery.

A wave of tiredness crashes into me, and I yawn. So much for working on the mysteries left by Zagan's visit. Tomorrow will be soon enough to determine an unknown demon's equally unknown victim. At least he gave me a clue, for all the good it does.

And there's still the matter of who killed Jenny along with who tried to kidnap me. Not to mention the way more pressing matter of how Zagan knows Eloise.

Yep, plenty of things to mull over tomorrow. Or later today, as the case may be. I should tell Smythe about Zagan's visit, but the sudden tiredness overwhelms me. I can talk to my mentor tomorrow about my personal demon appearance.

Letting loose with another yawn, I turn off the light and crawl under the covers, leaving the unanswered questions for when I wake.

Chapter Nine

Fingers tighten, squeezing my arm. My knees scrape along concrete as I'm pulled across the floor. The stench of puke and blood mingled with cleaning products assaults my nose. I can't move. I can't fight. A scream gurgles in the back of my throat, trapped by frozen muscles. I want to run. I want to escape. I want to kill the bastard who holds me captive.

I try to flail my arm, move my legs, but only accomplish a pathetic moan.

"Gin!"

The man holding my arm laughs. "Not close enough. No help for you."

"Gin!"

My arm shakes, my body trembling. Wicked laughter fades into background noise as another's fingers grasp my arm.

"Gin! Wake up!"

The command ricochets through my veins, a zinger of power laced in the words. My eyes open to a brow-furrowed Smythe. I sit, throw my arms around his waist, rest my head on his shoulder, and squeeze for all I'm worth. After a heartbeat's pause, he returns the hug, his hands making small circles on my back, letting me know without words everything will be okay.

His touch comforts, soothes, and chases away the dream.

"What was it?"

"A replay of last night." A shudder ripples across my skin. "Thank you for saving me."

One hand strokes my hair. "Always."

I raise my head, meet his eyes, our lips inches apart. His gaze bounces between my eyes and my lips as if asking permission.

Despite it breaking my personal rule, I want the comfort only he can provide.

He lowers his head while I raise mine, our lips meeting as one. Power surges along my nerves, my veins, straight into my core, a blossoming heat. He deepens the kiss as my fingers curl into his nape. So much for one little kiss. One kiss with this man will never be enough.

Wanting more of him, I lean back, and he takes the offer, pressing me into the bed, crawling up my body like he belongs, until he lies fully on top of me, the sheet a barrier between us.

Never releasing his lips, I reach under his t-shirt, trying to pull it over his head. I'm almost successful when his phone rings. He pulls back.

"You aren't answering that, right?"

Rolling off me, he pulls the phone out of his pocket. "It's work."

Well, shit. I throw off the sheet as he answers the phone. My body tingles in all the right places, eager for him to finish what we started. Too damn bad. I should've stuck with my personal commandment. Instead, I'm tingling, unfulfilled, and unlikely to get relief.

Double dog damn it.

Smythe white-knuckles his phone. Never a good

sign.

"Come again?" His brows drop low. "Why now...who else are you calling? Okay, we'll be there."

He yanks the phone from his ear and slams his finger on the screen, ending the call. Anger morphs into lust as his gaze runs the length of my body.

"I told you not to answer it."

He cracks a grin. "Yeah, well." His expression grows serious. "Maybe it's for the best. As much as I want"—he waves a hand in my direction—"we work together."

Not that it's stopped him in the past. A twinge of jealousy winds through my veins. He'll stop with me but didn't with his first mentee? Clearly, I read more into our abbreviated horizontal action time than I should have. Two choices, Gin, woman up and act like it's no big deal, or turn into bitch-zilla.

After a two second pause, playing nice wins. "It could get awkward."

He nods once, closes his eyes. When he opens them, only determination remains in their depths, his lust banked.

"The Agency has called an emergency meeting. That's what the call was about. Multiple demons have made an appearance over the last week, more than normal. No rise in crime, though. Those of us who can are going to meet to brainstorm."

Just what I wanted to do. Visit the Agency at its high-rise in Boston. My esteemed employer thinks I'm white trash. One of the other guardian mages, Samantha—whose perfectly toned body Smythe didn't mind sleeping with—tried to have me killed, not that anyone besides Smythe believes me. Smythe's father,

David—who oversees the guardians—belittles me at every opportunity. He belittles Smythe too, so maybe acting like an ass is just his personality. The whole building confuses my *justitia*, which is convinced a demon lives on the property, even though they say no demon has ever set foot inside the warded place.

Good times.

"Do I have to go?" Geez, can my voice get any whinier? It's like I've channeled a petulant two-year-old.

Smythe straightens his shirt. "Yes. Other *Justitians* will be there. You haven't met them all and should."

Oh joy. More condescending looks. *Look at the poor* Justitian *who didn't grow up knowing anything about this life and who actually has a job. How plebian.*

"I can hardly wait."

"Try not to be sarcastic."

"What do you expect? They all hate me."

"Not all of them."

"At least Samantha hasn't tried killing me lately."

"True that." His eyes flare as if he suddenly remembers something. "I know how she paid the minions she sent to kill you." He's at the bedroom door faster than the time it takes me to blink. "I'll be on my laptop. Get dressed." He shuts the door behind him before I can ask how.

I close my eyes, draw in a deep breath in hopes it clears my mind and release the breath on a sigh. Swinging my legs out of bed, I glance to the clock and blink in surprise.

2:00 p.m.? It's been years since I've slept this long. Years. Waste of a day.

Okay, not a total waste. Smythe plans on telling me

how Samantha managed to pay off minions to kill me. The thought of those minions reminds me of my friendly, neighborhood demon and the visit he paid me last night. Something I need to tell Smythe. Maybe he knows the identity of the person the mystery demon targets.

I pull clothes, a bra, and panties out of drawers before heading to the shower. Smythe didn't mention how long before we need to leave, but I plan on making the bathroom trip quick. More time to chat that way.

When I emerge from the bedroom, dressed and ready for meeting with the enemy, ahem, I mean my employer, the heady aroma of coffee greets my senses. Fresh, not the kind that's been sitting in the pot all day. Yummy. I love having a mentor who gets me.

I pour an extra-large mug, standing in front of the sink to sip the hot, liquid caffeine. Perfection. Rather like Smythe.

Gah. I really need to get him and our near miss out of my head. It didn't happen. It shouldn't happen. It won't happen.

Fake it until you make it.

"I found it!" Smythe shouts from the living room, mobilizing my feet into action.

Carrying my mug, I quickstep it next to where he sits on the couch, laptop resting on his thighs.

"What did you find?"

He points at the laptop, and I lean over his shoulder. "Proof Samantha did it. Well, almost proof. Still need to find the recipient of her transfer."

"You mean proof she hired minions to kill me?" Shortly after I started wearing the *justitia*, Samantha convinced me a hoard of minions were attacking in San

Antonio and I needed to help her ward fight. Which was a lie. Sure, there were minions in that park, but they had been hired by the blonde bitch to annihilate my ass.

Unfortunately for her, Smythe came to my rescue, burning the minions in an inferno of magic flame.

You'd think with evidence like that her toned ass would've been fired. But David took her side over mine. Only Smythe believed me.

And now he has proof.

"Yep." He thumps the screen.

"Is that Samantha's banking account?" At one time, watching Smythe break into websites worried me the feds would appear to arrest us for hacking. Now, I know better. Smythe's hacks were as commonplace as going out to eat and about as safe.

"Yep. With a large transfer two days before she kidnapped you." He points to the transaction. "I need to dig a little deeper and trace who the transfer went to."

"That's kinda stupid to transfer money when withdrawing it and handing it to the minion would've been less traceable." Goes to show being a guardian mage doesn't translate into having brains.

"Lucky for us she went with the transfer. I'll work on it when we get back from the meeting." He snaps the laptop closed. "We need to leave if we want to get there in time."

He places the computer on the coffee table and stands.

Time for the Zagan reveal. Yet another thing I have to, rather than want to, do. "There's something I need to say."

"Can it wait? We need to leave."

"Sure, but you won't be happy about it."

Smythe sighs, all long-suffering and half patience. He rolls his hand in a get-on-with-it gesture.

"Zagan visited me last night."

His jaw tenses. "And you're just now telling me?"

Heat slaps my cheeks as I remember his kiss. I clear my throat. "We were a little busy. And I really wanted to know how Samantha paid those minions."

He stares at me for a breath. "What did he want?"

"To let me know how upset he was about Bad Dye Job Guy drugging my drink. And to let me know about a rampaging demon out to ensnare a human. He said if we found the human we'll find the demon."

"Seriously? As if that is some new thing. Aren't all demons out to ensnare humans?"

"Yeah, well. I said pretty much the same thing. He kept insisting we needed to stop the demon by finding some mysterious human the demon targets."

"He's nuts. Oh wait. He's a demon. Same thing. That's all he said?"

"Pretty much." The part where he claimed my blood called to him, I keep to myself. No sense letting Smythe on to my past.

"Then we need to leave if we want to make it on time." One brow rises as he looks at my mug.

"What? They have a problem with this?" I hold up my mug.

He shrugs, the gesture implying they might. Too damn bad. Waking up without caffeine is not really waking up.

"Ready?"

He offers me a hand. Taking a deep breath, I grasp his warm palm. Time to face the esteemed Agency.

Chapter Ten

With his free hand, Smythe opens a portal. Several seconds later, we arrive in the white landing room of the Agency.

Smythe taps my mug, and steam begins to rise from the no longer frozen coffee. I offer him a smile before taking a sip. He gets me. I think I'm falling in love.

To the left of where we stand, teenaged geeks sit in front of a row of computers. As one they glance our way, their gazes returning to their screens after a two-count. I've been told the geeks are really mages in training who can stop a demon from transporting into the Agency. I've also been told this room is the only way into the Agency.

I'm not convinced on either point.

This group of teenagers, mages or not, fail to inspire any fear other than that they can hack into your email account. And I've seen Eloise portal right into the infirmary without a soul checking up on her illegal arrival. Not to mention someone stole my *justitia* from the vault where it had been kept after the Agency determined my ancestral line died out in the 1940s.

Clearly the Agency has security lapses it wishes to deny. Not to mention flat-out incorrect information.

If my ancestral line had died out, I wouldn't be wearing the bracelet, now would I?

After a quick nod to the teenagers, I follow Smythe across the room and out the door into a hallway decked out like a certain New York billionaire's apartment. Gold and crystal chandeliers line the hallway, plush white carpeting swaths the floor, dampening noise. The scent of lavender hangs in the air, tickling my nose into a sneeze.

"Bless you." Smythe glances over his shoulder. "You need a tissue?"

"No." I sniff. "I need this place to stop using lavender as air freshener."

"Sorry."

He leads the way to the end of the hall where the conference room is, but instead of opening the door and walking in, he hooks a right down another hall.

"What's wrong with the conference room?" I gesture over my shoulder toward the room where we've met before for a planning session, but he never breaks stride.

"We need more space. There's another room that's bigger."

Bigger? The conference room I refer to holds a table large enough to fill my living room and has enough chairs for half the city. How much bigger could this other room be? And if the Agency was this freaking rich, why couldn't they pay my salary so I could work full-time hunting the baddies?

A question they refuse to answer.

At the end of the hall, Smythe turns right, stopping in front of an elevator. When the door slides open, we step inside. He pushes the button for the eighteenth floor.

Like the hallway, gold gilds the elevator buttons,

lines the marble floor. Marble. In an elevator. Definitely an out-of-this-world experience. The door pings our arrival, opening into yet another decked-out hallway. We step out, following voices around a corner to the obvious meeting place. Smythe nods at the huddle of bodies so I mimic him, wishing I knew who I was greeting. Not that it matters. A couple of waves and nods are all we get.

Smythe shoves open a door, and I'm snapped out of my thoughts into a full-fledged gawk session. Mirroring the other conference room, a wall of tinted windows overlooks the Boston harbor. Plush chairs sit in rows facing a podium with a projector screen hanging behind it. Almost all of the chairs are occupied with chatting people. Voices fill the space with noise thick enough to slice with a scalpel. A few people at the back turn when we walk in, but most don't notice us, continuing to talk as if they haven't seen each other for years.

Maybe they haven't.

I offer a smile to whoever glances my way as I follow Smythe to the nearest two chairs. Despite having worked with the Agency for the last three months, I only recognize a couple of the faces. The last time I met for a brainstorming session was when a group of mages led by Samantha raided Zagan's lair.

I take a sip as I glance around the room looking for Samantha. But I don't see her. Don't see David either.

"Where's your dad?" I gesture at the crowd.

Smythe's jaw tightens. "He'll be here. He's the one that called me."

"What's the deal with you two?"

He turns his head, his blue gaze piercing, urging

me to look at my lap. I refuse to take him up on the offer. I am not afraid of the big, bad mage.

Most of the time.

"Now is not the time to discuss that." The icy tone of his voice dares me to disagree.

Heat slaps my cheeks. Way to go Gin. Piss off your only ally in the room.

"Sorry. Didn't mean to upset you. I'm just curious."

His gaze stabs my soul like a knife, welling guilt instead of blood.

"Really. I'm sorry. I shouldn't have brought it up." I start to touch his hand, but he narrows his eyes.

"What happened to your father?"

Blood rushes from my face so fast dizziness swamps me. After I killed the wife-beating, child-abusing bastard, T talked to a ghost who helped us hide the body in a fresh grave in the local cemetery. The true reason T refuses to talk to ghosts. The reason neither of us will discuss.

We convinced the police dear old Dad walked out, deserting his family to begin another life elsewhere. Continued telling the story until his friends stopped coming around. Mom never asked. As long as the beatings stopped and the booze flowed, she accepted our lies right up to the day she died. Smythe, though, sees through our story as if he read the truth from my mind.

Which as a telepath, he very well might.

I slam barriers around the errant memories, rounding them up, stuffing them into a dark corner where they seethe in silence looking for an escape.

My fingers tighten around the handle of my mug.

"I told you. He left."

"Uh-huh." He faces the podium.

I try not to sag in relief. A reprieve. For now.

Topic change time.

"What's on the agenda?"

"I told you." His voice ekes through tight lips. "An excess of demon appearances has us worried."

I swallow. "Right, right. I mean, what do they plan to do about it?"

"That's why we're here."

So much for a topic change. More like a make-Gin-look-stupid change. Wait. In this place, that's not much of a change.

Since Smythe no longer seems interested in talking, I glance around the room, looking for fellow *Justitians*. Which is harder than it seems. Not a one of them hops up and announces who they are. And the lack of demons in the place means no bracelets making a sudden appearance.

A door opens at the far side of the room, to the right of the podium, letting in some familiar faces—aka Samantha and David—and a not-so-familiar face. Instead of her normal black leathers, Samantha wears khaki pants and a white button-down blouse, both sculpted to show off her flawless figure. David looks the same as always, gray hair in a military cut, white button-down shirt, and navy trousers. The brown-haired man who walks in behind him towers over both Samantha and David with a physique like a cross between a body-builder and a rhino. His tailored dark suit shows off his bulging arm and chest muscles.

My *justitia* shivers, the silver links vibrating a warning. Nothing new there. The Agency gives the thing the creeps. Makes it think a demon exists where no demon could possibly be. I blame it on the white noise in the background. The sound drives me up a wall, why wouldn't it also bother my bracelet?

And then the thing completely misfires, jutting into a sword as if a demon or minion entered the room. Which, judging from the lack of reaction from the crowd, one did not.

Since when does my *justitia* misfire? Maybe it's not. Maybe a demon really does hide in plain sight at the Agency. What are the chances?

My mug falls onto the floor as the sword forms against the back of my hand, the bracelet links shifting around my palm to give the sword support. Hot coffee splashes against my pants, and I gasp.

Smythe's eyes widen, and several people around us turn.

I point the sword to the floor, trying to hide it against the inside of my calves. Talk about embarrassing. Anytime the thing wanted to return to its bracelet state would be nice.

Unfortunately, nothing happened.

Except for Smythe getting his surprise on.

"What the fuck, Gin?"

"No clue. It malfunctioned."

"*Justitias* don't malfunction."

I give the thing a shake, proving him wrong. Still a sword. With no demon or minion.

Un-fucking-believable.

"Do you see a demon or minion in here?"

"Don't be ridiculous." He shakes his head. "This is the Agency. It's warded against demonic intrusions."

"As I said, it malfunctioned."

Or did it?

"Thank you for coming today." David's voice booms across the room courtesy of the sound system.

The one good thing about his interruption? Most of the people staring at my wrist turn their gazes to the front of the room. Not that it helps my malfunctioning *justitia,* who continues to emit puzzled emotions through its path along my nervous system. Nor the coffee stain spreading on the no-longer pristine white carpet.

Smythe points a finger at the stain and mutters a word. I can feel the flash of energy as the spell erases the stain. Seeing how the noise level in the room dropped to nonexistent, I use telepathy to talk to my mentor.

Thought you weren't supposed to use a spell for something so trivial.

If it gets them to stop looking at us, then it's worth the energy.

I continue to face forward, like I'm paying attention to whatever it is David says. *What the hell is wrong with my* justitia?

No fucking clue. Try telling it to retract.

Closing my eyes, I locate the purple entity of the *justitia* lying along my nerves and ask it to stand down.

Demon? Despite not having a voice, its bewilderment comes across as if it shouted.

We're at the agency. No demon. You can retract.

Demon?

No freakin' demon. Retract!

If it had been a teenager, the damn thing would've rolled its eyes and spat out a "fine." With a pop the juvenile equivalent of shooting the bird, the sword retracts into the bracelet, the silver links rattling as if I missed the message it wasn't happy.

I remove my arm from between my knees and straighten as if nothing happened. The people around us have stopped looking at me and are focused on David like he's passing out winning lottery tickets to one lucky soul.

Good job. Smythe pats my knee, never removing his gaze from the front of the room.

Yeah. But we still need to figure out why it did that in the first place.

After the meeting. Look sharp and pay attention.

Yes, oh mentor.

He shakes his head while removing his hand from my knee. I should be paying attention, but the room's congregants provide a shiny distraction. Which ones are my fellow *Justitians*? Which are mages? Why does my *justitia* think one of them is a demon?

What's going on in the Agency to give my *justitia* the demon-spotting jollies? I'm no longer convinced it's the staticky white noise puzzling the thing. Is it possible a demon could get into the building?

Were there even doors opening from the sidewalk?

I'd never been outside the building, but what were the chances of no outside doors? Wouldn't that be a fire-code violation?

"...Gin Crawford."

My name leaving David's lips snaps my thoughts out of their questioning loop. What the hell did he just say?

Pay attention! Smythe's voice explodes in my mind. *He commended you for killing two demons.*

Thank you. For saving my ass yet again.

I give a little finger wave and a shrug. Which are good enough for David and everyone else staring at me. Gazes heavy with curiosity and suspicion return to the front, leaving my cheeks warm.

Head out of your ass, Gin. Pay attention.

"The other *Justitians* are killing more minions than ever. Crime has increased worldwide. Terrorism. Murders. Kidnappings. Rapes. There are too many of them and not enough of us. We need a game plan. A way to send them back to Hell where they belong."

Whistles and claps sound in response to his good-guy anthem call. I'm beginning to feel like a super-human from one of those comic-book-based action movies. Go Team Agency!

David nods at the audience before bringing his hands up in the well-known meeting gesture of settle down. "Chuck Tweedy has some ideas on accomplishing this goal."

He steps back and the brown-haired, muscle-bound man steps forward. Cue the clapping. Even I get in on the palm-slapping action, mainly to look like I fit in.

Who the hell is that?

Smythe raises a brow. *The leader of the Agency.*

I thought that was your dad. Wasn't the leader of the guardian mages the leader of the Agency?

No, Dad is the leader of the guardian mages, which makes Chuck his boss.

So your dad is second in command?

Something like that. Try to pay attention this time.

As you wish. I wink at him. Pat his knee. Wish I could run my hand up his leg…

Gah. I really need to stop thinking of Smythe in that way.

Which is about as hard as bringing a DOA back to life.

Chuck air pats his hands, asking for quiet. The low rumble of his voice fills the room. "Thank you for coming. I know you are all busy. First and foremost, we need to get a handle on these attacks. We need to discover why they are occurring and put a stop to them."

I tune him out as he drones on and on, reiterating David's good-guys anthem speech. Yes, yes, yes, there's a lot of shit going on in this world and not all of it is human-based. What else is new?

Cynical much?

"…offense instead of defense. We need to find their lairs and attack them there. Samantha here"—he points to her, as if we can miss her—"led a team against Zagan. They went to that demon's lair and annihilated his ass. We need to do more of that. We need to share more intel. Work together instead of separately. Any suggestions for doing so?"

Hands shot up. Impatient people shouted. And the room turned into a high-energy buzz of excitement.

I lean over to Smythe, pitch my voice low. "Seriously? Does he really expect us to come up with that answer?"

"Why not? Maybe someone has a better answer than him. We aren't a dictatorship."

"I don't want to work with anyone else on a daily basis. Working with you is good enough for me. Why add another?"

"That might not be what's decided."

"I guess teaming up with others on occasion is okay. It's just doing it all the time that bothers me."

He smiles. Instead of the knee pat, he grabs my hand, lacing our fingers together and giving a squeeze. Then he sets our joined hands on his thigh. My heart trips a fast beat. My breath hitches in my throat. The noise of the room fades away until the only sound left is his heartbeat and mine, a fast dance of attraction.

In the middle of a meeting. With a roomful of people.

Not our smartest move.

I look at him, at his profile, while he faces forward. He squeezes my hand again, his grip loosening, when I see a flash behind him, out the wall of windows. A helicopter flying over the Boston bay draws closer, and I lean forward to watch. Tightening my fingers on Smythe's, I give our hands a little shake.

"Look at how close that helicopter is flying to the building."

Smythe turns as the thing flies parallel to the wall of windows, hovering above the ground. Chuck stops speaking, which means heads start turning to the helicopter.

And then all hell breaks loose.

Chapter Eleven

A door on the side of the helicopter opens, allowing the muzzle of some huge-ass machine gun to stick out. Before I can ask if the wards are set to stop gunfire, the gun explodes with a steady stream of bullets. Glass shatters. People scream. Smythe yanks me to the ground, falling on top of me as if his body wards off bullets.

My *justitia* tightens, releasing on a sharp sting as it changes into a sword. Too bad I'm lying on it.

Screams, shouts, and spells mix with the loud thuds of bullets smacking into walls, ripping through flesh. The thick coppery scent of blood fills my nostrils. I swallow, trying not to gag.

Bloody bodies lying on exam tables in the ER don't bother me. Active crime scenes? The stench of fear mingled with the acrid scent of blood turns my stomach into a nausea-inducing machine every time.

Silence descends, punctuated by the *click-click-click* of a jammed gun and the moans of the injured and dying.

Smythe jumps to his feet, along with other mages, hands held toward the helicopter as they shout spells. Energy builds in a line, an invisible wall replacing the shattered windows. Just in time for the gun to un-jam and the shooter to start firing.

Bullets smack into the mages' invisi-wall and

bounce off. Score!

Right when I push to my knees, a bullet smashes through the magical wall, takes out one of the mages. Shit! I yank on Smythe's arm, get nowhere, and ram my body into his legs. He stumbles, rights himself against a chair. More bullets crash through the barrier, despite the mages sending extra energy into the thing. *Pop!* A flash of light in the invisi-wall indicates a bullet breeching the barrier.

Smythe shakes a leg, trying to dislodge me, but I have a brother and know how to tackle. He falls against the chair, a combo of shock and anger racing across his face. I grab his arm to yank him down beside me and get nowhere.

His mouth opens, but before he can yell at me a series of *pop, pop, pops* coat the room in terror. The barrier keeping us safe from the gunfire flickers under a barrage of bullets. And then it and the remains of the windows explode into the room, glass flying as sharp projectiles, the blast knocking us backward like ships tossed in a hurricane. I bounce off the back of a chair and land in a heap by Smythe. My ears ring loud enough to turn the constant *bang-bang-bang* into a dull background noise. Everything hurts, but a quick body systems check proves no serious injuries.

Blood drips down my arm as I roll onto my stomach, small cuts from the glass turning my arm into a macabre splatter painting. It hurts. I ignore it as I inch toward Smythe. Tiny slices streak his face, but that injury isn't what catches my eye. A large glass shard pierces his chest. Dark red blood blossoms from the wound. Gunfire erupts over our heads as I use my free hand to explore the extent of his injury.

Not good. Without help, he could bleed out.

My gaze snaps to his pale face. Keeping one hand over his wound, I give his shoulder a shake with the other, but his lids remain closed.

"Smythe?" No response. "Aidan?" Still nothing.

A shot of panic ricochets through my body. Why won't he wake? Excessive blood loss? Which did not bode well for him. I touch his bare arm and a well of silent darkness pulls me into its depths, his normal thoughts absent.

How bad was he hurt?

"You better not die on me, you hear?"

Still no response. I withdraw my shaky, blood-coated hand.

His blood on my fingers draws memories of a dead Blake from their hiding place, a wellspring of emotion bubbling through my veins. Dark red fills my vision, drives my anger. A rushing noise fills my ears, blocks all remaining sound in the room.

Those minions are going down.

And I'm the one to kill them.

Without thinking, I rush the shattered windows as if I'm one of those super-human action heroes on the big screen. Thrusting the sword before me, blade facing the attackers, I run forward, my yell heard over the *pop-pop-pop* of the gun. Which, of course, trains on me as if spotting an easy target. Yanking on the red energy Zagan filled me with after my fight with the fear demon Agramon, I throw it around me like a bulletproof coat until I glow with unholy power.

When I get to the former wall of windows I stop. I might be charged with some extra enhancements, but I'm pretty sure flight isn't one of them. Gathering the red energy into my palm and along the *justitia*, I shout at the minions in the helicopter.

"Go away!" Real original, but it's the first thing that enters my mind.

Naturally they crack smiles. Then I let loose with the ball of energy while pointing my sword at the gun. My energy ball strikes true, smacking the minion manning the gun in the chest. The minion flies backward out the opposite door of the helicopter, falling to the ground. The gun explodes into pieces.

The pilot's eyes widen. I reach inside for another round of energy, but he yanks the craft up. The steady *thump-thump-thump* of the rotors fades as he flies off.

I collapse. Apparently throwing Zagan's red energy drains me of mine.

"What the fuck did you just do?" David's voice penetrates my ringing ears.

Oh shit. Turning into the equivalent of a human glow stick was probably not the best move for keeping secret the source of all that red power.

"Killed a minion?" I shove to my feet. Always best to face the devil head on.

Not that I stop to chat. Stumbling into a run, I head to Smythe, David following in my wake. When I get to Smythe, his eyes are closed, dark lashes contrasted with his pale cheeks. David gasps, shoves me out of the way, and kneels by his son.

I give my wrist a shake and command the *justitia* to turn back to a bracelet. With a shiver of the silver links, the thing obeys me. I kick a chair out of my way and kneel beside Smythe. Taking his wrist in my hand, I check his pulse. Thready and weak with skipping beats, a definite symptom of blood loss.

At least he's alive. For now.

"Don't just sit there. Do something!" For once David's gruffness doesn't bother me. His wide eyes and trembling hands speak louder than his words as to his shock and horror.

Emotions we share.

Before I can move, shouts herald the arrival of the healers.

"Who needs help?"

"Who's hurt?"

"Who's injured?"

David stands. "Get your asses over here now! What the fuck took you so long?"

One healer jogs over, medical bag strapped across her chest. Brave woman to run straight for a scared and angry father.

She doesn't ask questions, just kneels beside Smythe, unzips her bag and pulls out a wad of gauze.

"Hold this." She directs, passing me the gauze.

I press the gauze around the shard, doing my best to ignore David who hovers over her shoulder as if to critique her work. In my ER, we would have run an IV with fluids, typed and crossed him for a blood transfusion, and called the attending doctor to determine if the wound could be fixed in the ER or if he had to be transferred to the OR. Instead, the healer holds her hands several inches above his wound and mutters words that sound suspiciously like Latin.

A blue glow surrounds her palms as she places them on either side of the shard.

"I can move if you need the space."

She shakes her head, continuing whatever spell she speaks. Smythe draws in a deep breath, which I take as a good sign. After a couple of tense moments, she stops muttering her spell.

"Pull the shard out slowly."

I grab the piece of glass and tug gently. She resumes her spell, continuing when the glass pulls free. I drop the bloody thing on the floor, then grip Smythe's hand. By this time David has inched around the healer to kneel at Smythe's head, his hands stroking his son's hair as if he's a small child.

"The bleeding's stopped." The healer fists her hands, the glowing blue light dying. She rocks back on her heels to stand.

"Where are you going?" David snaps his gaze to the healer. "He's not awake."

"There are other injured. I've done all I can for him. You'll need to either wait for an available stretcher or carry him to the infirmary."

David blinks, color rising in his cheeks like an impending storm. The healer holds his gaze for a two-count, then backs away, clearly wanting out of the path of the coming yell-fest.

"I've stopped his bleeding. Take him to the infirmary." And with those words, she hurries to the next victim.

Fists clenched, David watches her go, his glare strong enough to burst a person into flames. Good thing I'm not in the way of it.

Before he can incinerate the poor healer, I touch his hand, meaning to distract him, then offer calming words. Instead, I'm sucked into his emotions, into memories running through his mind. Red overlaid with orange tangle against a black backdrop. A woman lies in a hospital bed, hooked up to a ventilator, her pulse a steady *beep-beep-beep* on the machine monitoring her vitals.

David yanks his hand away, the image vanishing. Who was she? Not that I'm going to ask. He looks pissed enough to fry me where I sit.

Back to the original goal of calming words.

"His bleeding has stopped. That's good." That burn-me-up glare lessens as I talk. Thank God. "Let's pick him up and take him to the infirmary. Okay?"

A swallow followed by a nod, and David takes Smythe into his arms, heading for the door. I never would have pegged David as being strong enough to carry the six-foot-five giant otherwise known as my mentor, but he doesn't even grunt or strain.

Maybe he cast a strength spell. If there is such a thing.

We pass healers working on the injured. I should help, should put my kickass ER nursing skills to good use, but Smythe takes priority. What would I do without him?

Healers and injured line the hallway, interspersed among debris. The once-elaborate hall lies in shambles, crystal chandeliers shattered, the pristine carpet smothered with blood. David hooks a left out the door, passing by the carnage on his way to what I hope is a shortcut to the infirmary. The only way I know of to get there is from the landing room.

The man might be gruff, get on my last nerve, and be the poster child for an asshole, but he loves his son. Which means there has to be an infirmary shortcut up ahead.

And sure enough, a cluster of healers dashes toward us pushing stretchers.

David snags a stretcher and places Smythe on it with care, ignoring the wide-eyed expression of the healer shoving it. Clearly, the thing was meant for someone else. Not that the healer objects. For once I want to high-five David.

Instead I help him push the stretcher down the hall, the healer following behind like a dog wanting its toy back. We turn a corner to a bank of elevators. I hit the up button and pray the elevator hurries.

Smythe has not woken. His wound no longer bleeds, but he should have at least opened his eyes. Or moaned. Or something to let us know he's going to be okay. My chest aches, my breathing coming in short bursts having nothing to do with pushing a stretcher down a hall. I grab his hand right as a beep lets us know the elevator arrived.

We shove the stretcher into the elevator, plastering ourselves around the sides, backs against the walls. Whoever designed this elevator needed to ride in it with a stretcher and medical personnel. Maybe then they'd have widened the thing.

A ding indicates we've arrived. Once the doors open, the healer guides the stretcher to a vacant bed.

"Help me get him into the bed. I need to take the stretcher back to the conference room."

As soon as we transfer Smythe to the bed, he grabs the stretcher, racing back the way we came.

"I'm gonna find someone. Stay here." David points at me before turning on his heel, his footsteps lost in the noise and excitement.

This time when I touch Smythe's arm, his sleepy emotions tumble into my mind. Under normal circumstances, he'd be blocking my attempts to read him. Provided it was one of those rare times he actually let me inside his mind. His emotions circle around, vultures sighting prey, struggling to fight, to win. Win what, though? The lost minion fight? A battle over death?

A light brush against my arm snaps my thoughts out of my mentor's head. I look up into Eloise's blind, red eyes.

"Thank God you're here."

"It is not God that sent me. What happened?"

I open my mouth to answer, but David strides into the room, worry written in the white lines bracketing his mouth.

"No one is avail—" David catches one look at Eloise and pauses midword. He blinks. Swallows. "Eloise?"

"David." The coolness in her voice deepens my curiosity as to what lies between them. Maybe nothing. It could just be David's "loving" personality finding another fan.

"Are you available to help Aidan?" His voice roughens around the edges, like a person who has lost a precious item only to be told it's been sighted.

Eloise stiffens. "I would not be standing here if I was not. Now, please, tell me what happened."

As before, I assume she does not mean the attack, per se, but how Smythe sustained his injury, so I answer accordingly.

"The mages formed a shield, but the bullets managed to take it out. Then there was this blast, and the remaining window glass shattered inward, and we all went flying. That's why he's cut. He had this huge shard in his chest"—I point at where the glass ripped into him—"that one of the healers fixed. She got the bleeding to stop, but he still won't wake."

"Hmm. Move out of the way." She gestures to the foot of the bed, exchanging places with me.

Unlike the other healer, Eloise does not mutter a spell under her breath. She moves to Smythe's head, places her hands about an inch off his skin, and forms a blue light with her palms. The light travels down his body, reversing course when it hits his boots.

Eloise sucks in a quick breath, her eyes widening.

"What?" David barks.

"Quiet." Her tone brooks no argument.

David closes his mouth, but tension racks his body. In contrast, I relax, my breathing no longer coming in short gasps. As the recipient of several Eloise healings, I know she's the best around. I'm pretty sure she can bring back the injured from the edge of death. I'm living proof. She can do the same for Smythe. He's in good hands.

Literally.

Not even her quick jolt of surprise worries me. Whatever is wrong with Smythe, she can heal it.

I expect the small cuts on his face to heal. But they don't. My breath hitches. I refuse to give thought to the knowledge in my head. Blasts can give rise to bad brain injuries.

Nope. Not going to dwell on that thought. It's bad enough the idea popped out of its hiding place. And it shouldn't matter. Eloise is here. Eloise will heal him.

Right? But what if she can't?

And as quick as a second, my breath catches in my chest, the short gasps making my vision swim. My heart pounds as if I ran a marathon.

Get a hold of yourself, Gin. He'll be okay.

He will be. He will be. He will be.

I chant those three words over and over again until they are the only thing I hear.

After what seems like an eternity, the cuts on Smythe's face begin to close, the scabs fading into smooth skin. David releases a noisy breath, obviously as relieved as me.

I knew she would heal him. Never doubted for a minute.

The second doesn't count.

Eloise sends a wave of blue energy down Smythe's body, but this time it wraps him in its light until he glows like a blue LED. His breathing evens out, deepens, as his muscles relax. Eloise steps away from the bed.

"Don't touch him. Don't move him for at least twenty-four hours. He should sleep most of that time."

"What was wrong?" David asks.

"Bleeding and swelling of his brain. I corrected the leaks and dispersed the swelling. He is lucky I got to him in time."

David nods, his gaze caught on his son. Since he doesn't tell her thank you, I should.

"I'm glad you were here." I reach for her hand, but she pulls it toward her. Right. Whatever's in her mind she doesn't want me to see.

Weird. I know she can block me like Smythe does, turning my empath ability into nothing, making it so I can touch her without reading her emotions.

What changed?

"You are injured." At her words, David's gaze snaps off his son and onto me.

I glance down my body. Yep, definitely injured. Amazing what a dose of adrenaline can do for a person.

Small cuts decorate my arms, my legs, my torso, turning my clothes into a palette of different shades of red. Yet another outfit destined for the trash.

One more reason not to come to the Agency.

"I didn't notice."

David's clinical gaze rakes my body. It's then I notice, while I'm sliced and diced, David still wears an almost-pristine white shirt. The only blood on his clothes comes from his son. Not a scratch on the man.

He either forms a wicked shield or something is seriously wrong with this picture.

"You should have noticed. It's not too late."

I raise a brow at the healer's words, I can't help it. Is Eloise referring to my cuts or my thoughts about David?

"Well, don't just stand around, Gin. Let her help you. We can't afford to lose another *Justitian*. No telling how many were hurt in there."

Oh my God, almost all the *Justitians* were present in the conference room when the gunfire and blast happened. Were they okay?

"I've got to go help—"

"You need to sit and let me heal you." Eloise gestures to the bed next to Smythe.

"Someone else might need it."

"Sit the fuck down." David points at the bed, his anger slithering across my skin like a snake.

Cold seeps into my marrow, fright riding my thoughts. I do as he says, obedience ingrained from childhood. Once my butt hits the bed, a shot of anger chases away the chill.

Damn it. I know better than to be cowed by the likes of him.

Eloise touches my arm, apparently no longer afraid of my skin. Nothing happens. No glimpses into her mind. No bells or fireworks. Nothing but the cool dark space indicative of one used to blocking thoughts.

"Close your eyes. This won't take long."

Considering my choices are do as she says or continue dripping blood on the infirmary floor, I close my eyes. Within seconds, I'm floating on a bright blue ocean of healing, idyllic white clouds drifting above me. Peace settles my nerves as I drift on a wave of bliss.

Chapter Twelve

A touch on my cloth-covered arm snaps me out of the ocean, landing me in the noisy infirmary. Jealousy surges. I actually wish I was Smythe, injured enough to require more than a few minutes drifting in peace. Then my brain kicks in, naming the jealousy for what it is: stupidity. I feel great, hyped on energy, powerful, why botherwith the green-eyed monster?

Now that I have wayward emotions settled, I open my eyes. Eloise stands before me, fingers touching my clothed upper arm, the cloth shielding me from her thoughts.

"Better?"

Does she ask to be polite or a lack of self-confidence? I vote for politeness. No way could she have gotten this far in life without realizing she's the best healer around.

"As always. You rock."

One side of her mouth kicks up. "I'm needed elsewhere. I'll return to check on Aidan."

Those words she speaks to David, who nods in understanding but says nothing. Jerk. I answer for him.

"Thank you."

She nods, steps around David as if he's an obstacle in her path of life, and disappears into the crowded room. David stands at the foot of Smythe's bed, arms crossed, eyes narrowed.

What's he mad about now?

He's staring at me as if I did something wrong. But what?

He wouldn't answer even if I asked. And while his general attitude and lack of injuries might make for a conversation starter, other items take precedent.

"I can help triage in the conference room. I've been trained for this." Well, not exactly for minions shooting up a roomful of mages and *Justitians* per se, but definitely for multiple casualties.

"What made you think you could stop the minions?"

Huh? Shouldn't he be telling me to get my ass in the conference room and help? Not to mention I really don't want to get into why I was able to throw red demonic energy at minions.

Some knowledge is better left secret.

"Isn't that my job?" My raised brow is intended to be scathing enough so he stops asking questions. It fails.

"I'm referring to how you took them out."

"I dunno." I shrug, all nonchalant in hopes he misses the tremble in my limbs. "I just did." I'm such a good little liar.

"You fucking threw red energy. Like a demon. Are you so dense you didn't notice?" He takes a step toward me.

Now it's my turn for narrowed eyes. "Are you accusing me of siding with the enemy?"

"I don't know? Should I?"

"I can't believe you even went there. I refuse to discuss this with you. Since Smythe isn't waking anytime soon, I'm going to go help."

David interrupts my storming off by grabbing my upper arm.

"You aren't going anywhere until you explain." His grip tightens.

I freeze, prey to his predator. Damn it. I just told myself I'm better than to fear him. Stuffing my annoying fear reaction deep inside, I glare at his hand, shift my gaze to his and drop the tone of my voice.

"Let. Me. Go. Unless you want a scene?"

He drops my arm. "This isn't over until I say it is."

Bad villain much, David?

Straightening my shoulders, I offer him one last glare before marching to the elevator, my limbs trembling with too much adrenaline.

Does he suspect? Clearly, I'm dense to even ask. Of course he suspects. Else he wouldn't have become so angry. I shove the down button while glancing over my shoulder. David's calculating gaze strikes me with the charm of an enticing cobra.

And once again I'm frozen to the floor, eyes wide and heart pounding.

Damn it. I really do know better than this.

"Gin?" Eloise's voice snaps my head around. She stands several feet behind me and to the left, partly hidden behind a privacy curtain. "If you aren't busy, we could use your help."

Ding! The elevator beeps an arrival notification. I glance between it, David, and Eloise. Eloise wins. Giving my back to David while ignoring the beckoning escape hatch, I walk to the healer.

"Whatcha need?"

"It's not much, but we could use a hand in here." She sweeps aside the curtain, ushering me into the alcove made by a circular metal track on the ceiling holding the aforementioned white curtain.

A young Asian woman lies on the bed, attended to by a blushing female healer. Her chin-length, jet black hair frames a pale pixie face, her dark gaze slicing the poor healer into strips of embarrassment. Blood streaks the patient's dark blue long-sleeve shirt and jeans, another victim of the shattering glass. The healer holds the woman's hand, turning it back and forth, allowing the light to catch off the silver links surrounding her wrist.

A fellow *Justitian*! Another sword sister. Only the third I've met. The first, Micah, died shortly after we were introduced. I saw her replacement only once from a distance. And now this woman.

I turn to thank Eloise, but she's vanished, lost in the storm of incoming victims.

"Hey." At the sound of my voice, the woman turns to me, her dagger-sharp gaze a hard strike.

"Hello?"

The healer glances at me, relief flowing across her face as if she sees my interruption as her ticket to leave. "That does it for now. Someone will be back to check on you later."

I nod to the healer as she hauls ass through the curtain, but the *Justitian* remains close-mouthed. Until the curtain falls behind the healer, leaving me and my sword-sister alone.

Her eyes narrow as she shoves upright, balancing on her elbows, legs reaching toward me. "I remember you." A slight accent tints her words.

Impressive. She speaks my language, and I couldn't even tell you what country she's from.

"You are the one who defeated the minions. How did you do it? I have never shot red lasers at minions."

Neither have I, but if she wants to label demon energy a red laser, more power to her.

"I'm not sure." Liar, liar. "It just happened." Which is mostly true. I've only used the energy twice before in my fights with Agramon, the demon of fear. Both times drawing the energy from its hiding place inside me seemed harder.

Third time's a charm?

"I would like to learn."

"I'm not sure that is a lesson I can teach. I can't describe where it came from." Truth. I will never, ever mention to anyone—other than possibly Smythe—who filled me with energy.

Nope. That little secret is between me and Zagan.

The expression on her face falls as if I stole her last cookie. Guilt stabs my heart.

"I'm sorry." I am. Really. I would like to give the *Justitians* the red energy. Imagine the demon damage all thirteen of us could wreak using the demons' own power against them. Bwahahahaha. But no. Zagan wouldn't go for it.

And a small, insane part of me wants to keep the knowledge between him and me. He chose *me* to be the vessel for his energy. I need to keep my mouth shut about the deal.

Which is a little hard to do when I go throwing our little secret out in the open before a crowd of freaking mages.

Good lord, what was I thinking?

"You look disturbed."

Yeah? Ya think? "Sorry. I keep replaying the

attack in my mind."

She nods. "That happens. How do you call it? Bad experience disorder?"

"Post-traumatic stress disorder."

"Yes, yes. That's it. All of us get that. Memories replaying."

"I guess it's better than the alternative."

One fine brow rises. "Yes. That does not help when you see the memories."

"I know." I swallow, dropping her gaze. Some memories should be forgotten. Time for a topic change. "I'm Gin, by the way. Gin Crawford."

She nods. "Pleasure to meet you, Gin. I'm Wu Cong, but you can call me George."

"George?"

She shrugs one slender shoulder. "I like the name."

Okaaay. "Nothing wrong with George." I shift from one foot to the other in the pause following my comment. "Do you come here often?"

"You truly are new."

"What does that have to do with the question?"

"You should know the answer."

"Color me a newbie."

Her brow furrows, smoothes. "Newbie? Does that mean new?"

"Yeah. Yes. Sorry."

"It's good to learn. To answer your"—she pauses—"newbie question. No, I do not come here often. We rarely all gather in one place at one time. I live at the Agency in China."

"There's an Agency in China?" I blink, as if that will help erase the stupidity gurgling inside.

"Newbie." Her lips turn as she straightens, plumps

the pillow, and leans against it. She gestures to the bed, and I perch on the edge. "You do know there are thirteen *justitias*?"

"That I do know. Mine's the thirteenth and had disappeared until I found it." Stuck my hand into my scrub pocket at work and pulled out a bracelet. Sounds like a bad nursery rhyme.

"Where was it?"

"My *justitia*?"

"Of course. It disappeared. Where was it?"

How much should I tell? Was it a secret? What harm could it be to share my story with my fellow *Justitian*?

"I'm a nurse in an ER. One day a minion attacked one of our doctors, my friend Will. Will was the doctor, not the minion. Anyway, I found him after the attack, and the *justitia* appeared in my scrub pocket. Will had it originally, although how he got it is somewhat of a mystery. I mean, his parents, specifically his mom, gave it to him when he was a child, but he never realized the significance of it."

A wrinkle forms between her fine brows. "Good story. How did it get into your pocket?"

"I don't know." I shrug. "Will said he wanted me to have it but can't remember putting it into my pocket."

"He lived?"

"Yes. Turns out he's a mage."

Her eyes widen. "A mage? Perhaps his parents stole it?"

"Maybe."

"But why? Why would you steal a *justitia*? Only one of its bloodline can wear it."

124

I shrug. "Who knows?"

"Did he know he was a mage?"

"Not until we told him."

"Was he downstairs during the attack?"

"No." Unless she asks, I'm not volunteering that Will refuses to learn mage skills. Something in the set of her jaw and the calculating expression in her dark eyes tell me she won't respect his decision.

"Most interesting. Legend has it your *justitia* was locked in a secure vault."

"That's what I've been told." A secure magical vault impossible to break into. Or so they thought. Turns out it wasn't so impossible after all.

"It should not have disappeared. Or turned up as it did. A mystery for both the disappearance and the reappearance." Her eyes narrow as she drums the fingers of one hand against her leg.

"What do you think happened?" I've already told her my suspicions, which echo Smythe's. Time for hers. Maybe she can think of something we overlooked.

"Clearly it was, how do you say? An inside job?"

I nod.

"Magical security in those vaults. All the buildings have them."

"All the buildings?" My mind continues to reel with the knowledge the Agency possesses buildings throughout the world. A fact which should have been told my first week of employment.

Yet another important detail the Agency forgot.

She huffs. "Yes. All."

"How many is that?"

"Five."

Five. Five Agency buildings in the world. Five

large buildings a new employee should have been told about. What the hell is wrong with these people? How can an employer overlook important points like its size when on-boarding a new hire?

Granted, being informed I was the world's newest demon huntress wasn't exactly the same as being hired for a job, but still. An employee handbook sure would have been useful.

George waves a hand. "As I was saying. Magical security means little risk of items in the vaults being stolen. Very safe. Your *justitia* should be in the vault, not in some doctor's possession."

"What do you think happened?"

"As I said, inside job. Someone wanted it. Gave it to the doctor's parents. Or maybe they stole it. Why, though?" She taps her pursed lips with one slender finger.

"That's the question we can't figure out. Perhaps the thieves believed it wasn't safe in the vault."

"Nonsense. You can't get safer than a magical security vault."

"The black market?"

"For *justitias*?" She laughs. "Only the bloodlines can wear them. There is no black market."

"I suppose not." A thought pops into my head, dark and scary. One I prefer to keep to myself: the thieves stole my *justitia* to keep it from falling into the wrong hands. The wrong hands in this case being demonic. Zagan told me enough to make me realize the bracelets were forged deep in the bowels of Hell.

By demons.

Perhaps those same demons want their bracelets back.

Have I told my suspicions to Smythe? I can't remember. My guess would be not likely. Some things Zagan tells me, or in this case hints at, are best kept between the two of us. Although I try to tell Smythe most of what Zagan tells me to help build the trust between mentor and mentee.

I can't help keeping our secrets. My *justitia* considers the demon a friend, and friends don't roll on each other.

"You look thoughtful." George interrupts my musings.

"Sorry. Just trying to come up with another reason. You've gone through the same reasoning my guardian and me have."

"Where is your guardian?"

"In a bed undergoing healing. We're not to disturb him for a day. What about yours?"

"Same. He was injured saving me." Her gaze drops to her lap, lips whitening with her memories.

I touch her jean-clad leg. "I'm sorry. What did the healers say?"

"I'm healed. We should have brought our own instead of relying on yours."

"What's wrong with ours?"

She raises a brow. "American healers aren't as good." Smugness tinges her tone, bristling my nerves.

"I have no problems with them."

"You are new." She shakes her head, dark eyes glittering with an unknown emotion. Pity? Disgust? Either way, my proverbial hackles rise.

"Eloise is the best. She heals me all the time." Self-righteous bitch. How dare she stomp on—what seems like—my personal healer.

Curiosity slides across George's face. "Who is she?"

"The white-haired, pale-skinned blind woman who told me to come see you?"

Her nose wrinkles. "I have not seen this woman. That would be hard to miss."

"She opened the curtain"—I point at the curtain surrounding the bed—"and called to me to see you. When your healer was in here?"

George shakes her head. "The only healer here was the one you saw when you opened the curtain and said hello. That healer was not your Eloise."

Okay. Now I'm a little freaked out. Eloise clearly called me over here. She disappeared right after, which wasn't too unusual. But for her to never have been here?

What. The. Hell?

"I saw her." My voice holds tones of a too-tired toddler on the verge of a breakdown.

"And I say she was not here. I would know if one of her type came in here."

"Her type?"

She waves a hand. "You are upset. Go. Find your healer. I will be here if you want to return."

I clamp my lips together before saying what I'm sure to regret. Instead I nod and slip out the curtain. I stand by the curtain breathing in deep, trying to calm the wave of anger crashing through me. How dare George say those things about Eloise?

Breathe in and release.

Okay, Gin, if you were in her country wouldn't you rather Eloise work on you than one of George's healers? Wouldn't you defend her skills?

Definitely. Wasn't I already? Yep, yep. So how can I blame George for doing the same thing?

Logic might not chase away the anger, but at least it manages to lessen the irritation.

Chapter Thirteen

The infirmary bustles, the elevator receiving a workout. Almost all the beds are full, healers rushing from one curtained area to the next, checking on victims. Eloise is nowhere to be seen.

Which might mean nothing except she is treating a patient.

Or it could mean…what, I don't know. Did I imagine her by George's bed? How could she have been there and not be seen by George?

Or was George lying? I scratch that thought as soon as I think it. What reason would she have to lie?

"Excuse me!"

I step to the side to avoid being hit by a fast moving stretcher carrying an unconscious mage. Standing in the middle of a bustling infirmary might not be the best place for a thought-fest.

Fast-stepping to where Smythe lies, I inch back the curtain to take a quick peek inside. He continues to sleep, but the best part is David no longer sits by his son's side.

Gin?

Hurt mixed with sadness laces T's tone as his voice echoes in my head. What happened to my twin? I slip into Smythe's alcove, pulling the curtain shut for privacy.

T? What's wrong?

Jackie left.

That bitch. How dare she upset my twin? I've always thought T could do better than the Double D Wonder, but never imagined she'd dump his ass first. His loss envelopes me, a damp cloak of grief.

What happened?

She fell in love with Donny Football.

Come again? The idea of Donny giving Jackie more than an autograph and handshake baffles me into a fit of inappropriate chuckling. I clasp a hand over my mouth, as if that will keep the laughter out of my telepathy.

She fell in love with Donny Football.

Yeah, that's what I thought you said, but I'm having trouble understanding why she'd leave you for him.

Ditto. A visual of him pacing in my kitchen, beer bottles lined up like soldiers on the counter, appears in my mind. Which I assume means he's drank all my beer.

Brothers.

What a bitch. I'm so sorry. Why would she think he'd return the attention?

No clue. But get this. She left to go stalk his house. She thinks he'll let her in and fuck her.

More walls, more walls. I will not laugh. I will not laugh. I don't want to upset T, but gaw-damn. The complete absurdity of Jackie and Donny...

A giggle leaves my lips before I can stop it. Geez. I can't help it though.

I'm sorry, T.

She left me for him.

Pain lances my right hand as T slams his palm

against the counter. Poor T. I need to stop chuckling at Jackie's attempted affair and focus on giving my twin emotional support. I rub my palm on my leg, dissipating the pain, while I talk.

She's a ditz. You know she doesn't think things through. She'll be back when nothing happens.

She betrayed me. I don't want her after this.

Cha-ching! Another thought I wall off quick.

I'm sorry.

No, you're not. But that's okay. I'm beginning to see why you didn't like her.

I try for an encouraging edge to my voice, hoping it doesn't come across like I'm dancing a happy jig. Which I'm not. Dancing might disturb Smythe.

You can do better. Double D's only get you so far.

That's not the only thing I liked about her.

Better you know now than learn later she's cheating.

He pauses, his whirling thoughts blowing through my mind like water vapor, dissipating without becoming tangible. *Maybe I should go after her, you know? The cops might arrest her for stalking.*

That's her decision, not yours. No, no, no. Don't go get Jackie. Please.

I don't want her to get hurt.

I know you don't, but I really don't want you to get caught for stalking her either. She left, no matter how stupid she is, she left. Don't go chasing after her. That makes you look desperate.

He pauses. *She's not stupid, but yeah, you're right. I'm just...I thought we had something.*

The tone of his voice pulls on my heart. My poor twin. Jackie was a ditz, and T could do better, although convincing him of that truth never worked. Love strikes in odd places. I should know.

I'm at the house. When will you be home?

Not until tomorrow. I'm at the Agency, and there was a minion attack.

Holy shit, Gin. Anger coupled with terror banishes his sorrow. *Are you okay?*

Yeah, but Smythe's not. Eloise healed him, but he's going to be unconscious for the next day.

I told you that fucking job would get you in trouble. You're lucky you weren't hurt. It's getting in the way of your life.

And in one millisecond I go from sympathetic to pissed off. Convincing him I enjoy my new gig, I like my *justitia*, I love Smythe's company, proves useless. I'm good at killing minions. I've taken down two demons, which puts me on par with several more experienced *Justitians*. Why can T not see how good I am in my new gig and how much I enjoy it?

My life? What life do I have outside of my job and Blake and he's dead?

Me! You aren't here for me!

I close my eyes and draw in a deep breath, anger dissipating as his fear over my possible loss lands like a punch to the stomach. Pain radiates from my heart to my limbs. My twin hurts. Therefore, I hurt.

I can't stand it when he hurts. Physical. Emotional. Both tear like a whip flaying against my soul.

T, I'm so sorry. I wish I could be there.

I know. I just...god, you were right, you know. I can do better, I just...yeah.

It's okay. You'll be okay.

He pauses. *You said Eloise was there?*

While I'm not at all surprised he asked, the idea of them together amuses me. *Why?*

Just making conversation.

Right. Subtle is not T's middle name. *She was here. Not sure where she is now.*

Tell her I said hi.

Sure. Because my new title is Matchmaker Gin. Time to hop back on the original topic. *Are you going to be okay?*

I'm always okay. His fake grin touches my lips like a ghost.

Seriously. Are you?

I'm upset, not crazed, Gin.

Good. Don't be. Crazed, that is.

Yeah, yeah. I'll let you get back to whatever it is you're doing.

Staring at Smythe? *Thanks. I'll see you tomorrow. It'll be okay.*

Yeah. I know. I just can't believe it ended this way.

You'll get through it.

I know. Thanks, Gin. See you tomorrow.

Love you.

Love you too.

He withdraws from my mind, leaving me tossed between happiness and despair. The blonde bimbo is gone, gone, gone. Happy dance time. However, my twin is depressed and scared over possibly losing me, which makes me sad. And the Agency was attacked, people were hurt, some were killed, and Smythe was injured.

Nope, definitely not feeling the happy-happy joy-joy.

Even if Jackie is out of my life.

Smythe's even breathing catches my ear, snapping me out of my thoughts. Thank God he lives. I wish I could touch him, but that would mess up the healing.

He's going nowhere, which means, I'm going nowhere. At least not out of the building. I should circle around to my original plan, helping triage in the conference room. Then I can find Eloise and quiz her about the disappearing act she performed by George's bed.

Help first. Twenty questions later.

Ready. Set. Go.

Chapter Fourteen

An hour later I'm back in the infirmary, the critically injured sent to beds or surgery, the dead covered in white sheets. Anger flows through my veins. Anger at the minions for their attack. Anger over my own sense of impotence. One mage died in my arms despite a healer's efforts.

Look on the bright side, Gin—most lived.

For once the bright side fails to impress.

If only I'd moved faster, stopped the minions sooner, the deaths and injuries would be less. At least the minion I blasted off the helicopter was caught. Not much left of him to question after an eighteen-story fall even if the demon essence animating him provided protection. Not much will be left of him either after the mages finish questioning him.

I swallow. Torture doesn't sit well with me. Despite its focus on a minion. Not that I feel sorry for the minion. Nope. The former human gets what it deserves. But it takes a certain type of person to purposefully inflict pain upon another, and I'm not that type of person.

I hope.

Taking a deep breath, I release my pent-up emotions on a heavy sigh. Now that I'm back in the infirmary, it's time to check on Smythe. I know he won't be awake, but I need to see for myself. To ensure he's still alive. I walk to where he lies and pull back the curtain surrounding his bed.

Blue light encases him in a peaceful glow. Dark lashes lay against cheeks beginning to regain color. An almost overpowering urge to touch him, to tell him without words what he means to me, strikes. My hands reach toward his leg before I stop.

What am I thinking? Eloise gave me a direct order not to touch him lest I screw up his healing session.

Speaking of Eloise. I need to ask her why George didn't see her when she stood right in front of my fellow *Justitian*. Cross that mystery off my list.

I turn, only to run into David, who apparently possesses ninja sneaking skills. He grabs my upper arms, not an ounce of his skin touching mine, as he stares into my eyes.

"Come with me."

"Okay." Did I really agree so easily? What is wrong with me?

The thought crosses my mind to disobey, to stay by Smythe's side, to tell David nope-not-going, but as soon as the thought appears, it fades. I want to follow him. I want to do whatever he says.

I want to grow a spine and break his compulsion spell.

Instead, like a brainless idiot, I follow him out of Smythe's alcove to the bed next to my mentor's. David opens the curtain and gives me a little push into the curtained room, right into Chuck, who sits on the edge of the bed. Not a good way to meet the Big Boss. The head of the Agency grabs me before I fall, hands careful to touch only my clothed arms.

My *justitia* squeaks, for my ears only, a mixture of

surprise and anxiety zipping through my nervous system. Silver links shift, as if to form a sword, but the transformation fails to complete. Thank goodness for that little blessing in this SNAFU situation. Why does it react this way to the Big Boss? What is it thinking? And why is Chuck here? Why am I? What nefarious plan is David hatching?

Why. Can't. I. Leave?

I try, God knows, I try. Although I can stand, shift from foot to foot, and scratch my nose, I can't leave. And man, I want to get the hell out of this partitioned area faster than Jackie dropped T for Donny Football.

"Have a seat, Gin."

I do as David says, sitting on the edge of the bed next to Chuck. Damn it. David uses the same compulsion spell Smythe uses, one of complete obedience. One I've not consistently learned to break. Smythe taught me the counterspell and insisted upon practice sessions, but did I learn?

Clearly not.

Time to dust off those lessons before I tell David what he wants to know: Zagan filled me with his power.

The words to the counterspell appear in my mind, tangled and underused. My *justitia* feeds me the spell one tongue-tangling word after another, until the counterspell flows like water through the canyon of my mind.

I can do this. Pretend I'm under the spell while spewing false information. I can do this. I can.

"Tell us how you got that red energy you used today."

I want to tell David, to confess how Zagan feeds

me power to defeat other demons. I want to. I know I shouldn't. I open my mouth.

"I don't know."

Pain slams into my chest, stealing my breath, racing my heart. It takes all my willpower not to gasp, not to blurt out my secret to stop the invisible torture. Within a second, my *justitia* shuts down my pain receptors, eliminating the breath-stealing chest ache. Even better, I remain passive, expression closed to the turmoil inside. I will never again complain about an entity living along my nerves. *Justitias* rock.

My gaze meets David's. His eyes narrow.

"You don't know?"

Another wave of compulsion washes over me, but I repeat the counterspell in my mind, and the inclination lessens. The ache in my chest isn't as great this time.

"No. I wanted to stop the minions, so I acted on impulse. The red light just happened." That much was true. When you yank upon power you possess, something usually happens.

"And you have no idea how you were able to shoot red energy?"

I want to tell him the truth. The compulsion beats against my mind, but another round of the counterspell lessens it.

I look David in the eyes. "No."

"She has to know." Chuck glares at me. "*Justitians* can't do that."

Maybe I'm different, sits on my lips, but I don't give voice to the thought. Am I allowed to speak without being spoken to while under compulsion? I can't remember. Even if I can, I doubt I should be able to sass the Big Boss. Silence is the way to go.

For the moment at least.

"That's nothing new with her. She came with extra abilities. Keeps my son on his toes."

I love it when David talks about me as if I'm not there. If it weren't for needing to play along with his damn spell, I'd set him straight.

"So you've said." Chuck's cold gaze leaves a trail of ice as it sweeps my body. "What about her bloodline?"

David shakes his head. "Our search hasn't narrowed down any leads. Aidan says her mother was adopted, but the records disappeared, so he hasn't been able to track down the birth mother."

According to the Agency, my *justitia's* ancestral line died out around World War II. So who gave birth to Mom? Perhaps I should show more interest in my genealogy, but who wants to discover their ancestry contains wife-beaters, alcoholics, and other crazies. Some things are better left unknown.

Clearly I need to rethink my tune. Only women of a certain ancestry can wear a *justitia*. Anyone else would not be able to access the bracelets' powers. And not only does each of the thirteen *justitias* possess its own bloodline, but only the women in a *justitia's* bloodline can access the power of that particular bracelet. So George couldn't wear my *justitia* and expect it to work.

Which means my history is more important than I want to believe.

And I need to pay attention.

"What about from our side? We keep records."

Another head shake from David. "Already tried that. No unexplained children."

"What about the secondary lines?"

"Same thing."

"I doubt you've had time to check all the lines. Think of how many there are."

"They were all checked when the primary line died out during World War II. Nothing. The entire line, primary and secondary, died. Then she"—David gestures to me—"appeared wearing the missing *justitia*."

Chuck opens his mouth, then shuts it as if he decided against speaking his thought. He glances at me. "We shouldn't be discussing this in front of her."

"She's spelled."

"Did you spell her not to remember?"

David grabs my arm, looks into my eyes, and I start reciting the counterspell as fast as my brain can trip over the words. He speaks, and my mind fuzzes, my consciousness focused on a recitation of ancient words. I refuse to forget, I refuse to forget, I refuse to forget.

My vision clears. I sit beside Smythe, watching as blue light coats his body in a healing spell. How did I get here? What happened between my counterspell and now?

Did I rat out Zagan?

At least I didn't forget the conversation between David and Chuck. But what happened next?

I yank out my phone and check the time. Only about thirty minutes since I came back to the infirmary from the conference room. Taking into account the conversation David tried to compel me to forget along with a couple of minutes before he found me, I conclude not much time lapsed from then until now.

Thank God.

I jump out of the chair and yank open the curtain between the beds. The bed next to Smythe lies empty, white sheet sans Chuck's butt print. So, I was out long enough for Chuck and David to remove all signs they were here. Damn it.

Wiping my sweaty hands on the curtain while closing it, I watch Smythe breathe. What happened in the few minutes between talking to David and now? Did I leak the secret source of my red power? I focus on taking deep breaths in an attempt to calm my racing heart.

If I had squealed, I'm pretty damn sure I wouldn't be sitting here. Nope. David would have hauled my ass to whatever jail the Agency possesses, not plopped me beside his son.

The logic sends a wave of relief through me. Along with a dose of pride. I thwarted David's compulsion spell. Go me.

What to do now? Track down David? Question Eloise? My thoughts circle around to David. I might want to track him down, but what would I say? I was supposed to be compelled into not knowing they talked to me. He might try another round of get-Gin-to-talk, pressing my luck at repeating the counterspell.

Eloise then. She can answer questions on how she disappeared without George noticing her and possibly put me to work while serving as an idea-bouncing board for all things David and Chuck.

Sounds like a winner.

Giving Smythe one last glance, I pull the curtain shut. The infirmary continues to bustle, but the franticness seems to have calmed a degree. Of course,

Eloise is nowhere to be seen.

Closed curtains line the row of beds, hiding the occupants from view. I walk the row, peeking into each curtain, finding plenty of injured, but no Eloise. No one asks what I'm doing or recommends me leaving. Lucky for me.

Except for when it comes to finding the healer.

Other healers and medics carrying medical supplies dart in and out of curtains, dodging around me as if I'm not there. By the second row of beds, I begin to wonder if finding Eloise ranks in the same category as finding a yeti. I might have better luck with the yeti.

Stopping where George was, I pull the curtain back an inch, but my fellow *Justitian* no longer lays in bed. Good for her. Wonder if her guardian made it out too? I hope so.

After closing the curtain, I walk down the last row of beds. No Eloise.

Damn it.

Now what? I can't go home. I don't have the key to Smythe's apartment. I refuse to ask David for a place to stay. No telling where he'd stick me.

A healer darts out of the nearest curtain, and I step back to avoid running into him, only to hit a body.

"I'm sorry." I turn, my eyes widening.

Eloise smiles. "Are you looking for me?"

"How did you know?"

"What did you want? In case you were wondering, tonight's planned poison detection training will need to wait." A small smile plays upon her serene features.

Poison detection training? My mind trips over that one for a second before remembering her promise to teach me how to detect poison in my drink. "Sorry, had forgotten all about that. What I want now is answers."

Her smile disappears. "In that case, here is not the place to find them. Come. We'll go someplace more private."

"Are you sure you can leave?" I gesture at a medic scurrying behind a curtain. "Don't they need you?"

"My work here is done."

I give her a slow blink, refusing to voice my thoughts. Since her blindness prohibits her from reading *the healing ward is much too busy for your work to be done for the day* expression smeared on my face, I hope she takes my pause for agreement.

One side of her lips twitches, a conspiratorial smirk. She grabs my upper arm, avoiding skin-on-skin contact. "Is there an empty bed?"

An empty bed? "Yes. Why?"

"Take me there."

I lead her to where George had lain, escorting her into the area, pulling the curtain closed behind us. "We're here."

"Can anyone see us?"

"Nope. I closed the curtain."

Her grip tightens as she circles her other hand above her head, forming a portal. The icy in-between swallows us whole in a breath-stealing gulp, then spits us out a second later in the living room of Smythe's apartment. While I stand mouth agape, Eloise drops my arm and walks to the kitchen as if she can see. Or maybe she's just that familiar with his place.

A stab of jealousy erases the shock of the portal. But only for a second.

"How the hell did you portal us from inside the Agency? I thought the building was warded against portals except for the landing room." Not that the wards have stopped her before. One time she portaled straight into the infirmary. Maybe the wards don't apply to healers.

Back to me, she shrugs. "There is much you don't know."

A pause permeates the room as I wait for her to finish her sentence. After a couple of seconds, I realize she is finished. Which tells me nothing useful. If I knew everything about the Agency, I wouldn't be standing here asking questions.

"Do you care to enlighten me?"

"Where to start?"

Another pause as she grabs a glass from the cabinet, filling it with water.

"Okay, I'll start first? With my questions?"

She turns, nods, raises the glass to me, and takes a drink.

Where to start, where to start? With the improbable portal or George? The vanishing act wins.

"Why did George not see you?"

"George?" Her brow furrows then relaxes. "You mean Wu Cong?"

"Yeah, the *Justitian* you wanted me to see. When I walked into her alcove, she said she'd never seen you, but you stood right there and told me to come in. How's that work?"

"She was distraught. Worried about her guardian. I did not perform her healing, so perhaps she did not notice me standing there."

"You're a little hard to miss." I cross my arms.

"Would you rather me say I erased her memory?"

"Did you?"

"No."

"Good."

"This is all?"

"Not even started."

"Then I should sit. Do you care for a drink?"

"Water, please."

She grabs another glass out of the cabinet, fills it with water, walks to me, and hands me the glass.

"Are you sure you're blind?"

Eloise laughs as she sits on the couch. She gestures for me to sit beside her, but I flop into the recliner.

"Yes, I'm blind. But if I know a person well enough I can almost see through their eyes. Not enough to see clearly, but enough to avoid obstacles. And this apartment is familiar to me. I know where the glasses are."

"How? I mean, I know how you know where the glasses are." She and Smythe are such good friends she's probably over here all the time. Or at least she was until Smythe starting spending most nights at my place. "What I'm trying to ask is, how do you see through another's eyes?"

She shakes her head. "That's my secret."

Oh well, it never hurts to ask. I give her a lopsided shrug. "Okay. Tell me why David's such a jackwagon."

"A personality defect?"

"So he was born that way?"

A distant look crosses her face. "Not exactly."

I circle my hand, encouraging her to talk. She takes a drink of water instead. Her eyes close as she speaks.

"His wife drank herself into a coma. She's currently in a nursing home. Didn't Aidan tell you?"

My breath catches. What a horrible thing to happen

to his mother. "No. He didn't."

"Hmm. I couldn't get there in time, and David has held it against me all these years." Her jaw tenses.

"But Smythe didn't?"

"No. He didn't."

"That's awful."

"I consider myself lucky Aidan did not hold me responsible."

"No, not that. I mean, that's good, but I was referring to the whole situation with his mother."

She nods. "If he has not told you, I spoke out of turn. Do not mention I told you. He is easily upset by his mother's condition."

"I won't say a word." My poor mentor. I can't imagine how it would feel to know your mother was technically alive but not be able to talk to her or have her aware of your presence. I hope I can keep the secret.

"Is that the only reason you wanted to talk?" Eloise raises a brow. "To ask why David is, how did you say, a jackwagon?"

I shift, leaning forward. "No. I had a run-in with him in the infirmary. He pulled me into the curtained alcove next to Smythe and spelled me to tell him why I fired red light into the minion 'copter. Chuck was there too. My *justitia* doesn't like either of them."

"You can fire red energy?" Her eyes widen. "That's—"

"Impossible. I know." One side of my lip curls.

"I am not the only one with secrets, I see."

"I'm just full of them." My grin falls short of crinkling my eyes.

"Yes. I am aware."

"What's that supposed to mean?" Surely she doesn't know Zagan gave me red energy?

"Darkness weaves through you. Some would care to exploit it. Or maybe they helped cause it." She taps two fingers against her lips. I raise mental barriers against my innermost thoughts as her not-so-sightless gaze turns to me. "Interesting. Very interesting. No wonder David tried to compel you. What do you think would happen if he learned your secret?"

I swallow. "He'd kill me."

"Ah, yes. Yes, he'd try. But not for the reason you think."

I'm pretty damn sure David would fry my ass, if he knew Zagan filled me with demonic red energy. No matter how I used the demon's gift. But since I'm not convinced Eloise wouldn't fry me either, I raise a brow and attempt innocence. Or stupidity.

"Whatcha mean?"

She taps her fingers against the glass. "You think he'd be mad at your perceived betrayal. But David possesses secrets I'm not yet ready to speak about."

"Then they aren't secrets if you know them. Which means you might as well tell me." I smile, encouraging her to spill her stash of knowledge.

A grin curves her lips as she peers at me from over the rim of her glass while playing the quiet game.

In-freaking-furiating.

"Are you going to enlighten me?"

"No. I already said that."

"What about Smythe? I mean Aidan. What does he know about all these secrets of his father's?"

"Aidan does not know many things about his father. We thought it would be better this way."

"Who's we?"

She sighs. "Gin, I want to tell you, really, I do, but I can't. Not yet anyway. But I will tell you much has been hidden at the Agency."

"No offense, but I already knew that. Figured it out my first day on the job. Tell me something I don't know." Tell me what else David is hiding.

"Okay. You are part of those secrets, that hidden information. Your being here frightens those who want to hide, those who seek to destroy. It's not just your newfound ability to shoot red energy that frightens them. It's the fact you exist at all."

My shocked gaze snaps from the glass in my hands to her glowing red eyes. Before I can ask her anything else, a wave crashes into me, and I'm floating on a gentle current, blue sky filling my horizon. Thoughts run through my mind, drift away in the warm salt water.

Eloise spelled me. Annoyance slams into me, only to float away. Like me, she protects her secrets. I can't blame her for spelling me into a dream state.

I guess she forgot there's always another day, another time we'll meet. Perhaps then she'll know how to answer, what lies to offer as truth. For I'll ask again. And again. Until she trusts me enough to tell the truth. One day she'll trust me. One day I'll learn all the secrets of the Agency. One day soon I'll discover what David hides.

But one truth I already know. Vipers fill the Agency, and David is the biggest one of all.

Chapter Fifteen

"Gin?" Warm hands touch my arm, give a little shake.

My eyes drift open, blink once, and again for good measure. Where am I? Memories sneak past a wall of sleepiness, filling in the gaps of my overly relaxed mind. Right. Smythe's apartment. Conversation with Eloise. A lack of resolution regarding David. Definite need for finding the healer for another round of twenty questions.

And something else. Something about Smythe. The memory floats out of reach before disappearing. If I was meant to remember it, it'll return eventually.

"Gin?" The fact Smythe stands next to me, warm hands giving my arm a little shake, hits with a shot of adrenaline, propelling me upright in the recliner.

A wave of dizziness rolls over me as I push to a sit. Sitting upright too quickly after sleeping is a bitch.

"Smythe! What are you doing here? You're supposed to sleep for a day."

"I did." His lips twitch. "It's Sunday mid-afternoon."

"Seriously?" Eloise magicked me into sleeping for eighteen hours? What the hell?

The lip twitch morphs into a full-fledged grin complete with eye crinkles as if he debates whether or not to laugh. "Yep."

I run my hands through my hair. No wonder I was so dizzy when sitting up. Eighteen hours of naptime will do that to a person.

"How are you?" I run a hand over the bare skin of his forearm, hoping for a reading, receiving only the cool darkness of a guarded mind. "You look much better."

"I feel much better. I'm lucky Eloise was there." He grabs my hand, runs his thumb across my knuckles.

A shot of desire sinks low in my belly. I squelch it and try to focus on the conversation instead of the fantasy playing in my mind. Bad Gin.

"Why wouldn't she be there? She's a healer. It's an infirmary."

"It's complicated."

"Complicated?" How complicated could reporting for work be?

"She's been known not to come when needed." His gaze grows distant. But only for a second. A sense I know what he's thinking pops into my mind only to vanish. "How many were hurt?"

I blink at his sudden topic change. Since I've been known to change a topic on rare occasion—okay, more like whenever I don't want to discuss deep, aka incriminating, thoughts—I give him a pass, filing the topic for another time. "Last I heard, ten dead, almost everyone else wounded."

"Dad?"

"He's fine." While I want nothing more than to broach the problem of David's lack of injuries with Smythe, now was not the time.

"Good. I thought he'd be there when I woke." His gaze drops to his feet, his voice pitched low.

I pat his arm, using my comforting nurse voice. "Last I saw him, he was close by."

"Why weren't you?" His gaze meets mine.

"Well…" I draw the word out, trying to find non-accusatory words to describe why I'm in his apartment instead of by his hospital bed. None exist, so I go for the exact truth. "Something happened with your dad, and I talked to Eloise about it, but she didn't like my line of questioning, so she spelled me into sleep. That was yesterday evening."

He blinks, a small wrinkle forming between his brows. "How did you get into my apartment?"

"Eloise formed a portal in the infirmary, and poof, here we were."

He drops my hand to take a step back, eyes narrowing in contradiction. "You can't portal inside the Agency."

"So you say. But you've seen her do it before. When she appeared in the infirmary after Agramon knocked us on our asses."

He runs a hand down his face. The couch squeaks as he sits. "She's not supposed to do that."

"Clearly she didn't get the message."

"I should've followed up with her sooner. I forgot."

"Is it that bad? Can your dad and other Agency leaders portal inside the building?"

"Wards are supposed to block all portals except for the landing room."

"Clearly, the wards aren't as strong as you thought. Or Eloise holds more power than they do."

Smythe shoots me a get-real look. "Eloise is a healer. Something's wrong with the wards. It's like they aren't working. The minions shouldn't have been able to break the windows in the conference room. Hell, their guns shouldn't have even splintered the glass. Wards coat this building against attacks. At least they're supposed to."

"Maybe it wasn't warded against bullets. You all normally fight with swords and energy balls, not guns."

His lips flatten. "The building is supposed to be warded against everything. Including bullets."

"Why don't you check out the wards? See if they're working correctly." Or not working as the case may be.

"That will take a couple of days. Longer if I try not to attract attention."

"You think there's a mole in the Agency." I don't need to read his mind to make that statement. The thought is written in the set of his jaw.

"Don't you?" He raises a brow.

"I've always thought there was something fishy in this place."

"I never noticed until you pointed it out when we started working together. I don't want you to be right."

"Of course you don't." Life would be so much easier if everything was on the up and up around the Agency.

Smythe sighs as he looks at his feet. "What did you mean when you said something happened with Dad?"

"It can wait."

His gaze snaps to mine. "That bad, huh?"

Holding his gaze, I debate whether or not to tell him. Who wants to know their father is a slime ball? How do I phrase that in politically correct terms?

I can't. Time for the truth, the whole truth, and

nothing but the truth.

"Your father compulsion-spelled me in front of Chuck. Tried to make me confess how I managed to take out the minion 'copter."

"You took out the helicopter?" His eyes flare.

Heat splashes my cheeks. "Um, yeah, about that. I guess you were out cold by that time."

"How'd you do it?"

Why did I open my mouth? Oh well, better he hear it from me than from someone else. "You went down. I got pissed, ran toward the helicopter, and the next thing I know I'm shooting this red energy at the minions. Knocked one out of the 'copter. The other flew off."

"Red energy?"

I shrug.

"You mean the same thing you fired at Agramon? Your eyes turned red then."

"I guess. It just happened." After I willfully drew on the power.

"I see. And how did you get this power? I thought your *justitia* redirected Agramon's energy."

I don't want to confess. I don't want him to think Zagan ensorcelled me. Most of all, I don't want him to know Zagan gives me power.

Being entrusted with secrets makes me feel important.

But I want Smythe to trust me.

Conflicted much?

"Gin?"

Right. Not answering the question is giving an answer.

I swallow.

"You're not going to like it."

"So I gather. Spill it."

I draw in a deep breath, release it as I speak dooming words. "Zagan gave it to me."

Smythe explodes from the couch as if a rocket of ire fired under him. "Goddamn it, Gin! What the fuck?"

He storms toward the kitchen, stops, and turns to me. I shrink into the recliner. But only for an instant. I am not afraid of the big, bad mentor.

I straighten my shoulders, stare him in the eye. "It's come in handy. My *justitia* had some help redirecting Agramon's energy. You didn't really think the bracelet managed to do that by itself, did you?"

He blinks, stopped cold in the face of reason. "Of course that's what I thought. You promised me you wouldn't blindly take orders from him again."

His words slice strips in my heart. Zagan once convinced me to lie to the Agency, to put on a show that made it seem like I killed him. Smythe saw through the charade. Although he kept his mouth shut, not telling the Agency the truth, his trust in me eroded. I've been trying since then to re-establish his belief in me, successfully until now.

"I'm not taking orders. He gave me this energy but never tells me how to use it. Remember, my *justitia* thinks of him as a friend, so why wouldn't he feel the same way about the bracelet? He's probably just giving me energy to help out the *justitia*."

"That's the dumbest thing I've ever heard. Are you listening to yourself?"

I cross my arms. "It's a plausible explanation."

"It's—" He pauses, a wrinkle forming between his brows as he thinks. "Why does Zagan think of your *justitia* as a friend?"

"He's never said." Neither has the bracelet. While it freely gives me snippets of memories and the occasional strong suggestion, conversations complete with answers are beyond its means. Which doesn't mean I don't have a theory.

Smythe reads my mind. "But you have a theory."

"Yeah. I do." And it's high time I shared the idea with someone. "The demons created the bracelets. Zagan created my *justitia*. Not sure why. Not sure how they came to be used against the very demons who created them, but that's my theory and I'm sticking to it."

His lips flatten, eyes narrowing. His mouth opens, closes. I keep my lips pressed together, letting him reason through my theory without additional help. After a couple of moments, he nods.

"Interesting theory. But if that's the case, why was that piece of history forgotten? You'd think the Agency would have recorded something that important."

"I didn't say I had all the pieces of the theory worked out. Only the idea."

"If you are correct, I bet it's hiding somewhere in the library. There're a lot of old books and scrolls in that place."

"Scrolls? You can't find it on your laptop?"

"Not all of the library's information has been digitalized. The Agency has been around for millennia. It takes some time to scan all our documents."

I nod. He draws in a breath, his gaze morphing from speculative to focused. And not in a good way. I squirm under the glare of his gaze, caught in a trap of my own design.

"This redirection won't help you, Gin. Nice

distraction, but the real problem here is you've hidden important knowledge. Why have you carried around a demon's energy without telling me?"

Can the recliner swallow me whole? Since the chair only squeaks under my squirming, refusing to transport me away, I give up on the plea. No getting out of this one.

"I know I'm sorry doesn't cut it, but I thought the energy would be helpful. And it was. You can't deny it."

Smythe rolls his eyes as if channeling a petulant teenager. "No wonder Dad tried to compel you. You told him, didn't you?"

"Don't be ridiculous. You're a better teacher than that." I sit straighter. "I kept reciting the counterspell, and the only thing he managed to make me do was forget a couple of minutes right at the end. He planted me in a chair by your bed, and he and Chuck disappeared." Go me. Again. I'm still in awe I managed to thwart David. On the other hand, a couple of minutes was plenty of time to spew secrets.

But if I told all, I guaran-damn-tee David wouldn't have left me sitting by his son's infirmary bed. Which means I rock at blocking counterspells.

"Huh. I guess you did learn something."

"Don't be so surprised. I'm smarter than you think."

"That's what worries me." He leans against the counter, arms crossed. "You infuriate me. Lie. Hide the truth—"

"Hey, now. It came in handy. We'd probably be dead if it wasn't for me."

"If it wasn't for Zagan, you mean. A demon, Gin.

A goddamned demon."

"He wants to help my *justitia.*" The words sound crazy even as I speak them. A demon helps a *justitia*, its sworn enemy? Maybe the bracelets were originally created by demons for whatever nefarious purpose, but they've since been turned against their creators. Why would Zagan want to help?

"Have you ever asked yourself why?"

Yeah, just now. "I didn't think about it."

"I know." His jaw tenses, relaxes. "And that's what's so infuriating. You act without thinking."

"Not all of the time."

"Often enough you do. It drives me nuts, but you're my partner, so I can't stay mad at you, either."

"And that makes you upset." I grin, hoping he really isn't as irate as he says he is.

He returns my grin, shoulders relaxing as if the anger holding him upright drained away. *Yes*! Mentally, I pump my fist in a victory dance. He's not mad at me. He forgives me.

I need to start telling him everything about Zagan, even the parts I prefer to keep to myself. Losing his trust in me is not an experience I care to repeat.

"I'm glad you didn't tell Dad. We need to discover the why of it before we go letting him in on your source of power. There's something about this whole situation I don't like, and I plan on getting to the bottom of it."

"And I'll be there to help you."

His gaze meets mine, draws me in, cements our pact. A sense of foreboding shivers along my spine. I ignore the possible meaning and stand.

"Are you ready to take me home?"

"Sure, but I need to come back to check out the

wards. And the library if I have time."

"Okay. I have to work tomorrow. Your Agency still hasn't hired me to do this demon huntress gig."

His lips twitch. "*Justitian.* Not demon huntress."

"So you say." I return his grin. "Ready to take me home?"

He holds out his hand, his palm an offer of peace after our fight, his grip strong enough to hold us through tough spots. And I want him to hold me, to stay with me, despite the secrets threatening to rip us apart.

Chapter Sixteen

Wednesday evening sneaks in early, darkness blanketing the wall of windows on the skywalk, making the hospital courtyard disappear from view. My feet hurt from running around the ER nonstop for twelve hours. Usually I get a break, but not today. Despite the lack of a full moon, the emergency room was packed with a variety of illnesses and accidents, dooming the staff to employ their iron bladders.

I've never been happier to see a toilet in my life.

An hour past shift end, I finally get to walk the long hallway leading to the parking garage. A set of double doors greets me at the end of the hall. I pull them open, the soft tread of my shoes against concrete lost in the vast space of the garage. The distant sound of a car starting echoes across empty parking spots, letting me know I'm not alone. Fluorescent lights buzz an uneven tune as I head to my car.

A shadow slips around my car. My heart pauses, resuming with a racing rhythm guaranteed to make a cardiologist reach for pills. Yellow fluorescent light turns the shadow into a man with dark pants and a hoodie, his face hidden in shade.

My breath catches. But only for a second.

The silver links of my *justitia* morph into a two-foot-long sword jutting across the top of my hand. Which, naturally, causes me to drop my keys.

Minion, whispers the *justitia*. *Kill.*

What a great way to end a tiring day.

Teeth flash white against tan skin. "Get ready to die, bitch. You ain't gettin' away from me tonight."

Was this Bad Dye Job from the club or a random minion with a grudge against nurses? I squint, trying to see his face above his upper lip. The voice was different, not to mention the guy from the club failed to set off my *justitia*.

Could this be the minion who killed Jenny? Chances are better it's Random Minion with a grudge.

"Sorry to ruin your evening."

The minion blinks, surprise radiating from his skin. Clearly, he expected me to run away screaming. The dumbass needs to check out the fancy sword jutting across the back of my hand. Maybe then he'd get the drift I'm not one to mess with.

Unfortunately, no such luck.

Minion takes a step toward me. I fall back into a fighting stance, flashing him my sword. The movement makes my purse slap against my hip. Damn it. I forgot about the purse.

Shrugging it off my shoulder takes only a second, as does pitching it to the side. But my gaze follows the purse instead of remaining on the minion. He uses the distraction to get in a punch.

Or half a punch.

I step to the side, so his fist grazes my chin instead of connecting with force. Evil thoughts skitter through my mind from his brief touch. Pain slithers across my skin, dull and infuriating. My *justitia* blocks my pain receptors. Euphoria slams into me as I duck down, ramming my shoulder into the minion's stomach.

With a loud "oomph," the walking evil falls onto his back, limbs moving like an upside down turtle, flapping around and getting nowhere fast. His gray eyes widen, face no longer protected by the hoodie's shade. A strand of light brown hair falls into his eyes, his tan sliding into paleness as he finally realizes I am his death.

A breeze laden with the salty scent of the ocean fills my nose as I raise my *justitia* for the killing blow.

"Good-bye, su—"

A heavy weight slams into my side, stopping my "good-bye, sucka" cold.

Concrete greets me with scrapes and bruises as I slam to the ground. No time to wallow in pain. The *justitia* takes care of the pain problem. Not to mention, wallowing on my back leads to whatever just hit me having a wide-open shot.

Demon, demon! My *justitia* shakes a warning, alerting me to the identity of my newest attacker.

I roll to my feet, albeit slower than normal. But that's what happens when the air gets knocked out of your lungs. The guilty party being a tall demon with dark hair and olive skin, wearing a blue polo with khaki pants. Like a taller, broader Zagan. A prickly sensation flows across my skin. As if I've met this demon before. As if I know him.

The strangest urge smacks me to stand straight, shoulders back, chin up, like a model showing her wares. Which makes abso-fucking-lutely no sense in the middle of a fight.

Although I made those exact same moves at my first night at Club Monster right after I saw a mysterious man observing me from the balcony. The emotions coursing through me now, the feeling I can conquer all, also occurred at the club. Could the man from the club be this demon?

I'd ask, but I'd rather concentrate on sending his ass to Hell where it belongs.

The creature stands in front of the slowly-rising-to-his-feet minion, palms facing me. Like it's protecting the poor little minion from the big bad *Justitian*.

Damn straight. This *Justitian* can whoop its ass.

"Do not steal what is mine, *Justitian*." The demon reaches behind, yanking the minion forward. As if there's a doubt who he means. He gives the minion's arm a little shake. "His deeds give me sustenance. You shall not take that away."

I take a step to the side, trying to circle around to get to the sustenance-giving minion. Kill the food source, kill the demon. But the demon moves with me, a proud grin parting his lips.

"You think you are better than me. You aren't. I am the best. And I will beat you." He flicks his fingers my direction.

A blast of energy slams me airborne, limbs pinwheeling in my best flying-ragdoll fashion. I land hard against the side of my car, breath once again knocked out of my lungs by the same guilty party as before. Which proves routine really can be painful. The minion laughs a spine-scraping sound, full of pleasure about my pain.

My *justitia* vibrates, happy attack tremors running along my arm, giving me confidence I can kill this thing.

The demon waves at the bright-eyed, maniacally grinning minion to stay put while he takes a step toward me. I take a step toward him, raising my sword to strike. A small finger flick is the only signal he forms a portal. I blink at the same time a pop sounds in front of me.

Before I can move, I'm slammed against the car by his hand at my throat. His other hand grabs my right wrist, trapping my *justitia* against the car. Pain slashes through my mind, his evil thoughts a swirl of horror. My *justitia* blocks the connection before my brain hemorrhages. Immune from his touch, I grab his hand with my left one and bring up my knee. Right before I make contact with his package of hellfire, he disappears.

After stumbling off balance, I right myself and turn in a fast circle. Where did he go?

This time he slams me face first into the side of the car, my nose crunching in agony. The *justitia* stops the pain but can't do a thing about the blood running across my upper lip. He traps my wrist with the *justitia* in a strong grip, holding both against the car. Once again my *justitia* blocks my empathic abilities. Cold anger rushes through my veins, fueling my muscles with adrenaline. I could call Smythe to help, but want to take out this demon on my own. It's up to me to escape.

"You aren't much of a fighter without your guardian."

Instead of offering a smartass comment, which is a little hard to do with blood running down the front of my broken face, I step on his foot, driving my sneaker into his instep.

He loosens his grip. I start to twist, but am rewarded for my efforts by another face-against-car move. Ouch, ouch, ouch. The *justitia* dials down the pain receptors and the empathic connection, thank God. At least I heal fast. Provided I get out of this fight.

Which I will. As if the alternative is an option.

The demon gives my trapped neck a little shake. His fingers tighten. Black spots dance along the periphery of my vision.

"Don't kill her. I want her." The whiny tone of the minion's voice grates worse than his crazy laugh. And leaves more chills.

On the plus side, the demon releases his grip. "She is not yours. But she can be valuable."

Damn straight. Provided valuable means not dead.

"I will let you live, *Justitian*. For now. You are"— he sticks his nose close to my neck, inhaling deeply as if he enjoys the scent of my fear-sweat—"attractive to me. We shall meet again. Tell your guardian Rahab gives his greetings."

The pressure against my neck releases as the demon's body moves. Footsteps followed by a tinny pop and a sudden cutoff of maniacal minion laughter let me know the demon-minion combo jumped a portal to Hell. Or wherever they crash at night.

The tiny pop of displaced air acts like a release valve, draining me of energy, my body collapsing next to my car while my heart beats an unsteady tempo.

That didn't go so bad. I'm still alive.

I wipe a hand across my bloody lip while checking for serious injuries. None of those, only scrapes, bruises, and a broken nose along with a side order of aches and pains. Everything will heal by morning. Quicker if I can get Eloise to come out.

Which she probably won't do for only a broken nose. And I'm still miffed at her for spelling me into an eighteen-hour sleep.

My *justitia* retracts into a bracelet after I give it an encouraging shake. I finger the silver links.

"Want to tell me who that demon was?"

Demon. Bad. Kill.

Yeah. Like I couldn't figure that out on my own. So much for carrying on a conversation with the entity living along my nerves.

With a sigh, I push to my feet, and retrieve my purse and keys. A quick hunt to the bottom of my purse turns up a tissue which I use to wipe my face. Taking a deep breath, I grab my nose, adjusting the bone back into place. As usual the *justitia* acts as an opioid, numbing the pain of resetting.

Good thing *justitias* can only be worn by certain bloodlines. Chronic pain sufferers would kill to own one.

Time to let Smythe know what happened. Since he dropped me off at my house on Sunday, I haven't heard a peep from him. Which is unusual. He said he was researching, and God only knows the man can research the hell out of the Internet, but he usually opened his laptop in my living room. This is one of the few times since we've worked together that he's left me alone for this long. Three days and I already miss him.

Not sure if that's good or bad.

Dropping my mental barriers, I use telepathy to call his name. T answers.

Gin? Are you okay? I sense pain.

A visual of T in a car flits through my mind.

Yeah, I'm fine. For the most part. *I'm trying to reach Smythe. He's not home, is he?*

I'm not home, so I don't know.

Where are you?

Tracking Jackie. She's at some club.

Which would explain why he's in a car. Since when is my twin one of those creepy exes?

T, stop being a stalker. Let her go.

Yeah, yeah. I know. But I can't. My palm stings from where he smacks his hand against the steering wheel. *I want to know if she slept with Donny. Then I'll leave.*

Oh, Lordy. *Call me if the cops catch you.*

Don't be ridiculous. I don't have to see him to know he rolls his eyes.

Since nagging him to stop his new stalker behavior will prove fruitless, I sign off to search for Smythe.

Later.

Bye.

He closes our connection, leaving me with a big helping of what-the-heck. That was strange on a number of levels. T's stalking issues aside, why did my telepathic skills default to my twin? Nothing to it but to try to contact Smythe again.

This time, I unlock my car, slide into the seat, locking the doors behind me. Because everyone knows locked car doors keep out demons. Yeah. Right. But the motion makes me feel better.

Leaning my head against the head rest, I close my eyes and locate the telepathic pathway Smythe uses. I trace it to an invisible wall ten feet thick. As I thought, he shut me out.

What's so important he can't answer my call?

The only thing left is to pick up the phone to call him. I bring up his number and hit the call button. He answers on the second ring.

"Yeah?" His tone indicates distraction. As if I caught him in the middle of a mentally taxing activity.

"Since you're blocking me, I'm using the old fashioned way."

He pauses. "Gin? You sound odd, what's wrong?"

I dab at my bruised, yet no longer bleeding, nose with the tissue.

"Nothing much. Just a run-in with a demon and its minion. Said his name was Rahab."

"What? Where are you? Are you okay?"

"You heard me. I'm in the parking garage at the hospital. And yes. Mostly."

"Hold on."

Two seconds later, a portal opens six feet from my car. I wave while pushing the end symbol on my phone. Smythe storms to my car as I hit the unlock button. He yanks open the door, concern vibrating the air around him with a righteous indignation.

"What the hell happened?" He grabs my chin, turning my face from side to side. White brackets form around his lips.

"Rahab said he let me live since he finds me attractive. Which is not a pleasant prospect. This was right after I almost killed his minion. I don't even know who the heck he is. Besides a demon who came to the defense of his minion."

"Start at the beginning."

I tell him about the threatening minion, how I almost killed the nasty before its demon appeared and tried to hand me my ass. The more I talk, the lower his brows dip.

"Rahab is the demon of pride. The leader of all pride demons. Being in his close vicinity rubs off on humans."

"Maybe that's why I acted like a cheap ho on display. It would definitely explain me thinking I could conquer the world." Or the demon in this case.

Smythe nods. "Could be. Still don't know why he showed up. Appearing in parking garages is not his normal modus operandi."

"I got the impression he came to defend his minion. But now that I've been introduced to him, I'm going to hunt him down. He's mine."

"That's my girl."

"But first I need to clean up."

He takes a step back, one arm resting on the open car door, the other on the roof, his gaze focused on my nose.

"I hoped you would be able to go to the club tonight. See if you can get a lead on that guy who tried to drug you."

"With a busted nose? Are you effing kidding me?"

His fingers tap against the roof. One, two, three. "We need to track that minion. We're not going to let your busted nose get in our way of stopping a killer. Your *justitia* will heal the bruising."

Mages and their singular focus.

Although, since I suspect I saw Rahab at Club Monster the other night, perhaps going there makes sense.

"Okay, fine. Either poof yourself over to my house or get in the car. I'm going home."

Smythe pauses as if he has something to say. After patting the roof twice, he gestures for me to get out of the car.

"What?"

"You're shaking. I'll drive you home."

I glance at my trembling hands. Yep. Definitely shaking. Good thing he offered to drive. Wait a minute. "You can drive?"

He shoots me a get real glare. "Of course. Just because I choose to portal doesn't mean I don't know how to drive. Now get out."

All righty then. I do as he says, walking around to the passenger side while he slips into the driver's seat. He pushes the seat back as far as it will go to make room for his long legs. I pull another tissue from my purse and hold it against my nose as he starts the engine.

His phone rings. He yanks it out of his pocket and slams it against his ear. "What?…It just now appeared on the computer? That's old news. We're already on it. It's hopped a portal back to Hell…Okay, you do that." He shoves the end button before sticking the phone in the cup holder. "Rahab just appeared on the Agency computer. So much for that demon identification program working in a timely manner."

"I guess something's better than nothing. Maybe a different programmer needs to take a look at it?"

"Not sure that'll help."

"On a different subject. Did you find anything on the history of the *justitias*?"

"My search in the library turned up nothing." He yanks the seat belt across his broad chest, snapping the buckle into place as if he possesses a grudge against the thing.

"Sorry to hear it."

"Yeah." He leans against the head rest with a huff. "Didn't have much time to look. Researching the wards took up most of my time."

"And?" I glance at him when he throws the car into reverse. He meets my gaze for a moment before shifting into drive.

"You were right. They'd been tampered with."

I knew it! The Agency should be a fortress impervious to a minion attack.

"How do you tamper with wards? Aren't they supposed to repel tampering?"

"Good question. Yes, they are. But they didn't. Someone with enough juice cast a breakage spell, which lowered their ability to repel intruders."

"Intruders like armed minions."

"Yeah."

I nod. Until another thought strikes.

"Speaking of, why can't the minions just walk into the building? Why bother with the helicopter?"

"The entrance is for show. Spells turn away curiosity seekers. Non-magical people pass the Agency, see it as another old building and leave it alone. Why?"

"Something I thought of during the attack."

"Your mind works in mysterious ways, Gin."

"Thanks for the compliment."

His lips turn in mirth. "Who says it was a compliment?"

"Uh-huh. Back to the wards. What else did you learn about them?"

"That's it. Someone tampered with them. Or maybe several someones. The warding spell is difficult to cast, even more difficult to break."

"Could the same person who cast the spell break it?"

"My understanding is the original caster died years

ago. Others strengthen the wards. Bottom line, it's not just one person who helps ward the Agency."

"Who's strong enough to break the spell?"

Smythe pauses. After a few breaths I risk a glance at him. Jaw tense, he stares straight ahead. His fingers flex and release. Rays from the streetlight strobe light, dark, light across the angles of his face.

"Charles Tweedy."

My gaze returns to the road as a wave of sympathy crashes into my chest. Smythe doesn't need to deflect attention from the real culprit. I know who, even if he refuses to admit it.

His father.

Chapter Seventeen

The space in front of my house sits empty when we turn onto my street. Surprise strikes hard and fast, dissipating as my brain kicks in gear.

T left to stalk Jackie. I really need to put a stop to his new extracurricular activity before he gets arrested or slapped with a restraining order. I never in my wildest imaginings pictured my twin stalking his ditzy ex-girlfriend. He never bothered with his other exes. Besides the double D's, what makes Jackie so special?

Good thing Smythe wants to go to the club tonight. I can kill two birds with one stone. Maybe three, if Rahab appears.

Smythe hits the clicker, opening the garage door. Once he puts it in park, he hops out of the car, slamming his door. He stalks up the stairs to the back porch, letting himself inside with a wave of his hand.

Locks are nothing to a mage.

Since tension filled the rest of the drive home, I assume my mentor spent his time wondering if his father was responsible for the dropped wards. While my father was a son of a bitch who got what he deserved, Smythe cares for David. God only knows why. David snips at him, belittles him, and acts like an ass to everyone.

Talk about your dysfunctional relationship.

Maybe one of these days he'll let me in on why. Or

not.

With that thought, I slam the car door to follow Smythe inside the house. The sound of fingers tapping on a keyboard greets me as I close the kitchen door.

Ah, the wonderful sounds of home.

Ignoring a feet-propped-on-the-coffee-table Smythe, I duck into my bedroom, drop my purse on the bed, and dart into the bathroom.

I stare in the mirror at caked blood smeared across my chin. Looks like I missed some spots when trying to clean my face in the car. Perhaps Smythe ran into the house to escape my appearance as opposed to feeling guilty about David. I touch my achy nose, not too surprised the expected bruising failed to appear.

Lucky me. Being a *Justitian* has its advantages.

I wash my face free of dried blood and take another peek in the mirror.

While the *justitia* eliminated the bruising, it has yet to get rid of the swelling. Puffy skin rings my nose, creases under my eyes, giving a new definition to bag lady. This I can work with. Remembering makeup tricks from my abusive past, I pull out foundation, along with varying sponges. Five minutes later my face is back to normal.

I continue applying makeup, highlighting my eyes until they pop with color. Good enough for the club. For a brief second, my imagination turns to Donny, to his laughing brown eyes, the way his arms squeezed my waist as we danced. He'd make some woman happy, if he'd settle down long enough to keep her. Just not me. I'd rather have the computer-geek mage typing in my living room.

Jackie better want a one-night stand.

Oh God, Jackie. According to T, she was going to the club in her quest to bang Donny. She might be a ditz, but she didn't deserve to be in the same club as a serial killer.

Provided the killer still stalked the club.

Yet another item to add to my long to-do list for the night. And here I thought convincing T to abandon the stalker game would be the highlight of the evening. Now I have to ensure his double-D ditzy girlfriend lives.

An idea teases me with what to do about Jackie. Have Smythe spell her into leaving the club. Excellent suggestion, if I do say so myself.

Satisfied with my game plan, I change from scrubs into the designer dress Smythe bought me, slipping my tired feet into the red-soled pointy heels. Good thing I had the dress cleaned since my last club adventure. When I walk into the living room, Smythe's gaze rakes my body from foot to head. A sexy smile turns his lips.

Yeah, he beats Donny on so many levels it isn't even funny.

I point to my face. "Can you tell I have a busted nose?"

He stands to walk toward me, his fingers gripping my chin with a light touch to tilt my head side to side. "A little puffy, but you did a great job with the makeup." His eyes narrow. "You've had practice."

Anger saturates the air around him, thick and potentially suffocating. At least it's not directed at me.

Shrugging, I turn my head, forcing his fingers to release my chin. "You ready?"

He stares at me for a second too long before nodding. Taking my hand in his, he waves his other palm, reciting his portal-opening words. We step into the in-between, landing in an alley by the club.

A deep bass pounds a rhythm into our chests as we walk to the club entrance.

"Don't drink anything."

I roll my eyes. Been there, done that, and refuse to try it again. I'm a quick study. "Not planning on it."

"We'll split up inside. I'll keep an eye on you."

"Just one?"

His brow furrows. "Huh?"

"Never mind. I'll look for the guy who tried to kidnap me. As well as stop T from stalking Jackie. Speaking of—"

"Wait. What's this about T and Jackie?"

"They split up. Jackie decided to make Donny her new bedmate. It's debatable whether or not he's onboard with the idea. T is madder than a wet hen and is stalking her."

"Good grief." He shakes his head.

"That about sums it up. He doesn't want her back, so I'm not sure what his deal is. At any rate, I thought maybe you could spell Jackie into leaving if you see her? I might not want her with T, but that doesn't mean I want her in danger."

"We'll see. If it looks like she's in trouble, I'll try to get her out of it. No guarantees."

"Gotcha."

I take a deep breath, giving myself an overdue mental shake as adrenaline floods my system. I have this covered. No drinking, which means the kidnapper won't have a chance at me. Nothing to fear. I can do this. I'm a *Justitian* with a super-cool bracelet and a sexy guardian mage.

I can do this.

Straightening my shoulders, I stride to the front door. No bouncer outside tonight. No line. Apparently Wednesdays weren't popular clubbing nights.

Smythe opens the door to show the bouncer waiting inside. He checks our IDs and with a jerk of his head ushers us into the club. Smythe squeezes my hand, opting for telepathy over screaming.

Take care.

See ya.

I give his hand a squeeze before heading toward Donny's room. Since Donny's bodyguard has yet to make an appearance, no telling if the star is here or not. I pause outside the door to the private suite.

What should I say? *Hello, here I am?* Or not bother with him, making rounds like I'm scoping the scene? I glance around the half-empty club, looking for T. I could use our twin telepathy, but part of me wants to be surprised if he's inside the club. Common sense beats out the small part.

T? I'm at the club where Donny hangs. Are you here?

Crickets answer.

T?

Either he's not here or he's ignoring me. I try hopping into his mind, but he blocks me. Okay then. He must be here someplace. Which means Jackie's here too.

Instead of hanging out by Donny's suite, I should track down Jackie and look for my attempted kidnapper. Although, chatting up Donny could prove advantageous. Smythe didn't say so tonight, but Donny still ranks up there on his suspect list.

Not on my list. I'm almost one hundred percent certain the football star didn't kill his fuck of the night and drop her body where he plays ball. He seems smarter than that. Or maybe I want him to be smarter than that.

No matter what.

In my playbook, he's innocent.

The door to his private suite opens. Donny pokes his head out.

"You standing out there all night, Gin, or are you coming in?"

I take a deep breath. Interview time it is.

Plastering on a smile, I give him a wink. "Just waiting for the invite."

He steps back to allow me to walk in front of him. I brush his chest with my shoulder as I pass. My *justitia* twitches, puzzlement ricocheting through my veins. A shiver creeps across my skin as Donny shuts the door.

Evidence too strong to ignore slams into me. I've written it off for too long, refusing to believe, refusing to accept. My jittering *justitia* only means one thing: Donny has cozied up to a demonic presence.

Chapter Eighteen

How can a demonic presence cover Donny like sludge without him becoming a minion? I stare at him for a second too long, activating the minion-trail sensors in my eyes, trying to determine why my *justitia* senses a demon presence on the football star.

No minion trails. No demon. No good reason for a shivering demon-sensing *justitia*.

Maybe it's malfunctioning?

Yeah, right. And maybe a pig's ass isn't ham.

"What's the matter, babe?"

Might want to stop staring at him as if he's a bon-bon, Gin.

I smile. "Nothing. Just a bit embarrassed you caught me lurking."

"Friends can't lurk." He winks. "Come on in."

Since the door is shut behind me, entering is my only option. I head to where Donny gestures, to the sofas lining the wall, the scent of beer and liquor enveloping me as I walk. I lick my lips as a memory of whiskey slides across my tongue. The remembered taste vanishes as I catch a glimpse of who sits on an overstuffed sofa dressed to the nines in a red low-cut blouse and black miniskirt.

Jackie.

Damn it. I was really hoping she wasn't here.

If hopes were dimes, I'd be rich.

A smile coats her face as she turns when Donny approaches. Until she notices me. I swallow a chuckle as her eyes flare, as her sexy pout turns hard. She glares at me when Donny sits beside her. Giving her a little finger wave, I settle on Donny's other side, sinking into the overstuffed sofa.

"Hey, Jackie."

"You two know each other?" Donny looks between us as if trying to guess where we met.

Obviously, he fails to remember meeting us at the post-game party. Must be one tackle too many.

"We do."

"Sorta." She responds at the same time.

Sorta? What the hell? She's been camping at my house for way too long to "sorta" know me. The bitchy side of my personality I try hard to keep hidden soars to front and center. Plastering a sappy, fake grin on my lips, I lean across Donny.

"T says—"

"Nothing. He says nothing."

Donny's gaze darts from Jackie to me, surprise at the oncoming catfight covering his face with an oh-shit expression. "T?"

"My brother. Jackie's—"

"Nothing. We broke up."

She glares.

I grin.

"Oh, right. My bad." I pat Donny's leg. "She's my brother's—"

"Ex. He's my ex because we broke up." She explains in a slow drawl as if talking to a small child.

I nod. I should close my lips since I don't want to say anything that might cause her to return to T, but dayum, a little revenge for my twin never hurt nothing. Right?

"He said it was so you could convince—"

"Honey, let's go dance." Jackie sinks her painted nails into Donny's thigh, leaning forward a bit to show off her cleavage. Which her blouse highlights like a glowing neon sign.

Donny's expression says he'd rather see where our conversation leads. As if he enjoys watching two women in a bitchfest. But the double-D's win out as Jackie stands, tugging on his arm. With a shrug followed by an apologetic look, he follows her out of the suite, leaving me stranded with five hunky players and their entourage of dagger-eyed fuck-bunnies.

Good times.

Since Smythe didn't take me clubbing for the atmosphere, I should get cracking on trying to find a killer and a kidnapper. Or maybe that person was one and the same.

A shiver courses through me. Being kidnapped was bad enough. Being targeted by a serial killer worse. At least my kidnapper was thwarted by Smythe. What made me a target? Talking to Donny?

"Drink, ma'am?" The woman server in a short skirt smiles.

"No thanks." After last Friday, no way in hell am I accepting a drink from anyone at this club.

Not until I determine who stalks the place looking for victims.

A sense of unease prickles my nape. Probably from the glares of the FBs in the room. Time to leave.

No one says anything as I walk out the door, the pounding bass covering the click of the latch. A quick glance to the dance floor shows writhing bodies bathed in pink and purple lights, but no Donny and Jackie. I edge closer to the dance floor as if that will help me see between shadows of bodies.

The same sense of unease I felt earlier returns. I turn, looking for a familiar face. Unfamiliar ones are all I see. Along with shadows, punctuated by strobing colorful lights.

If only the bad guys carried huge signs on their heads notifying everyone of their nasty status.

Although if they did, I'd be out of the demon hunting business.

Which bothers me way more than it should.

I circle the dance floor. Twice. Walk past the bar. Not only do I not see the guy with the bad dye job, I don't see Smythe. Or Donny. Or Jackie. Unease follows me as I walk another lap around the dance floor.

Why? Who or what causes that sense of being watched?

I stop near Donny's private room. Taking a deep breath, I close my eyes, tapping into my *justitia*. Perhaps it can identify why unease creeps across my skin like a rash.

Nothing happens.

Clearly the thing only works in the presence of demons and minions and not run-of-the-mill baddies.

"Hey, babe."

A squeak escapes me as Donny touches my clothed arm. My eyes pop wide to see him staring at me, a smirk twisting his lips.

"Geez, Donny, you scared the shit out of me."

"Sorry. You looked deep in thought."

My bracelet shakes another warning about Donny.

No good, no good, no good. Its thoughts circle around in my brain, confusion riding the words. Donny might not be a minion, but he's definitely been touched by a demonic presence, according to my jittering bracelet. But how?

"You seem…different."

His grin widens. "Good loving will do that to you."

I blink a couple of times as my brain sorts out that one. Did he mean…? "Where's Jackie?"

"Where I left her."

I circle my hand, urging him on. He rolls his eyes. "In the bathroom."

"Why…wait, never mind. I don't want to know."

"She really your brother's girl?"

"Not anymore. You met them." He gives me a blank stare. "Last week, at the after party."

Donny shivers, his gaze passing my shoulder. "Don't want to think about that or what happened to Jenny."

"Did the police tell you anything?"

"Naw, man, they cleared me. That's all that matters. Don't want to talk about it. You wanna dance?"

His grin appears again, leading me to wonder if "dance" is a euphemism for extracurricular bathroom activities. At one time in my life I'd take him up on his offer, but now? I'd rather have a six-foot-five-inch mage at my command.

I answer as if he means the dance floor. Because he might.

"My feet hurt too much to dance." I gesture to the writhing bodies on the dance floor.

Donny's grin widens. "Don't mean that kind of

dancing."

While I'm proud of myself for guessing his "dance" meaning correctly, I'm also a bit disgusted. How many times in a row can this guy get it up? That's a question I really don't want to know the answer to.

I touch Donny's sleeved arm. "Thanks for the offer, but no."

"You wound me." He clasps a hand over his heart. "It never hurts to ask a pretty woman. She might say yes." He winks.

You already had one say yes. How many do you need in a night? Geez Louise. My grin feels fake. "You know me well. Where did you say you left Jackie?"

"Second private restroom." He points. "Maybe I should go with you. My money's on you winning." He runs his hand up and down my arm. As if the motion will help change my mind.

"That's not necessary. I'm sure I can find her myself."

"Come see me when you're done." His conspiratorial wink produces the opposite effect.

Not happening, buddy.

"Good night, Donny."

Before he can say another word, I walk into the crowd, heading for the restroom he pointed out. Gross. Toilets are germy enough without adding anything extra. Wonder what T will do when he finds out about Jackie's tryst? Continue to stalk her? Beat up Donny? Nothing?

Not likely on the last point.

I push past drunk patrons until I reach the second private restroom. Part of me feels responsible for Jackie, which is ridiculous on so many levels. She's a

184

grown woman. I don't like her. I don't want her with my brother. Yet, I don't want her to be hurt.

And since that damn prickly feeling won't leave me alone, I'm concerned for her safety. What if someone stalks this club to target Donny's flings? Another dash of ice cold darts through me as I knock on the restroom door.

No one answers.

I push open the door. "Hello?"

Nothing.

No one is in the restroom except for me. Damn it. Where did she go?

Smythe? Have you seen Jackie?

A couple of seconds pass before he answers. *No, why?*

Donny just finished with her, but I can't find her.

Maybe she left?

I have a prickly feeling on my nape. And my justitia *senses a demonic presence on Donny.*

Fuck. Did you stab him?

Geez, Smythe, no. He's not a minion, but something has been near him.

It must be a strong demonic presence for your justitia *to pick up on it. They don't normally do that.*

What do you mean they don't normally do that? It's a demon-fighting bracelet—shouldn't it pick up on a demon presence? You know what, never mind. We can discuss later. We need to find Jackie.

Why?

Because I think she's the next target.

Why didn't you say so to begin with?

I thought I did.

He pauses. I can almost see him rubbing the bridge

of his nose in frustration.

What was she wearing?

A low-cut red blouse with a short, tight black skirt.

I'm looking.

While you're at it, look for an average-build guy with a bad blond dye job.

The one who tried to kidnap you?

Yep. Oh, and if you see T, holler.

Why don't you holler?

He's blocking me. Damn it. Did I really leak to Smythe my twin telepathic ability? Good thing he can't see the oh-shit look creeping across my face. Or feel my heart pounding behind my ribs.

Puzzlement tinges his words. *You do realize I know you and T talk telepathically, right?*

You know?

Until you learned to block me, I'd sometimes hear you two talk.

Oh God. He knows. He knows all my secrets.

What secrets, Gin? His voice whispers across sensitive neurons, firing them into a panic.

Throwing mental barriers around my secrets, my default mode takes over. Lie until you believe it's truth.

Nothing. Are you going to help me find Jackie or not?

He pauses. My mental barriers flinch as he tries to push through. Nosy man. I lean against the wall, using all my power to strengthen my mental defenses. He will not break through. *He will not. He will not.*

A tendril of irritation weaves through my mind.

We'll discuss this later. Take the left side of the dance floor. I'll take the right. We'll meet at the end.

I sag against the wall in relief. A reprieve. For now.

Doing as Smythe asked, I search for Jackie while avoiding servers and patrons. No Jackie, on the dance floor or off. Then again, the club possesses more shadows than lights.

Smythe stands at the end of dance floor, arms crossed, an avenging god on the warpath. Which does not bode well for me.

"I didn't see her." I pitch my voice to be heard above the music.

"Me neither."

"Got any magic tricks to locate her?"

"Not her, no. Let's search where I found you."

"Where's that? I don't remember much."

He grabs my hand, his grip adjusted more to holding a flailing patient than a strolling girlfr—I mean mentee. Leading me to a door close to the club entrance, he shoves his way inside to what is clearly a row of offices.

The music level diminishes as soon as the door clicks shut. A long hall stretches before us, punctuated on either side with closed doors.

I freeze one step inside the hall, my heart pounding a race beneath my ribs. This was where I almost died. Where some creep tried to kidnap me. Where Smythe rescued me.

My breath comes in little puffs, dizziness overtaking me. I sway.

Chapter Nineteen

I almost died here. In this hall. In this club. Small, shallow breaths lead to a crushing dizziness as my knees go weak. Smythe drops my hand, wraps an arm around my waist, supporting me as I sag.

"Gin? What's wrong?"

I manage to draw in a deep enough breath to chase off the blurry vision. After a couple of lung-filling breaths, I wave a hand at the buffed concrete hall. "I almost died here."

Smythe tightens his hold on my waist. "You were drugged, not dead. Big difference."

I pop him on the arm. One side of his lips kicks up. As if he wants to goad me. As if goading me will stop me from panicking.

He's cra—

My heart no longer pounds as if running a marathon. Damn it. He's right. As usual. Not that I'll admit it.

"Okay. Drugged. I thought I was going to die. So that makes it the same thing."

"If you say so." The one-sided lip turn becomes a full-fledged grin. But only for a moment as determination casts his face in lines. "What makes you think Jackie's a target?"

I push away from him, determined to stand on my own. My breathing normalizes as my heartbeat calms.

Score one for mage anxiety-calming powers.

Now for my explanation.

"It dawned on me, sitting in Donny's private room when she left with him, that the reason I was drugged was because I was with him. They had a, ahem, 'dance,' "—I use my fingers to draw air quotes around "dance,"—"in the restroom. If someone is targeting the women Donny 'dances' with, then maybe they would target her."

"You didn't have sex with him."

"No, but I was alone with him in his room. If someone was watching, they would've noticed me with him."

"Are you certain Donny didn't drug your drink?"

"Yes. Bad Dye Job Guy bumped into me before I started feeling wonky. Maybe he dropped something into my drink. It was after that I felt drugged."

"Maybe Donny put him up to it. There's something off about that guy."

"Jealous much?" I refuse to admit the thought has crossed my mind. I'm holding on to Donny's innocence with the tenacity of a cat caught in a tree.

Smythe shoots me a get-real glare. "You know it's a possibility. Just because you don't want it to be doesn't mean it isn't."

Busted. I sigh. "Okay. You might have a point."

"Might?" He raises a brow.

"Fine. You have a point. Donny didn't drug my drink. At least not that I saw. And Bad Dye Job bumped into me, which was a perfect opportunity to do the deed. It was after I ran into him that I felt drugged. Donny might have been around a demonic presence, but neither of them are minions."

"Jenny was killed by a minion. We saw the trails. As you said, the guy who tried to kidnap you was not a minion. Since when do minions hire humans to do their dirty work?" A line twists between his brows. "They prefer to do the deeds themselves."

"Maybe he's an odd one." I shrug. "Can we discuss this later? I feel like we need to find Jackie before someone else does."

"You still have that prickling sensation?"

I pause, assessing. "No. Not anymore. It's gone."

"Try T again. Maybe he found her."

"I can't believe you know we're telepathic."

"I can't believe you thought I didn't know." Humor fills his eyes. "Try him."

Closing my eyes, I reach for my twin. *T?*

Nothing.

A shot of panic traces through my system. He usually answers when I really need him to. Why isn't he?

T? Answer me, damn it!

After a long pause, a sense of irritation floods my veins, tenses my muscles as my twin finally reacts to my prodding.

What the fuck, Gin? I'm busy.

Finally. I sag in relief. He's okay enough to be angry. I can work with his temper.

Is Jackie with you?

No. I told you, she went to some club to find Donny.

And you were going to follow.

You were right. It was stupid. So I came back home. Can I go now?

My sisterly warning system hops into high alert.

What's he hiding? I try to push my way further into his consciousness, to see from his eyes, but he shoves back, prohibiting me from accessing his optic nerves. Which means my curiosity factor flies off the scale. *Whatcha doing that's so important?*

Nothing.

T.

He pauses, tendrils of irritation flowing through our bond. *Fine. Eloise is teaching me a spell. It takes all my concentration, okay? Will you let me go now?*

Uh, sure.

Too surprised to react, I stand frozen as he snaps his mental barriers closed. A big what-the-hell on so many fronts it wasn't even funny.

"Did you talk to him? Is Jackie with him?" The concern in Smythe's voice snaps open my eyes.

"Yes, I did, and no, she's not." I fight to hide the surprise from my voice. Eloise is with T? Words can't describe the emotions pinging through my mind. Oh, wait. They can. "We need to go home." I need to see this for myself.

Smythe shakes his head. "We haven't finished searching the club."

Leave it to my mentor to stay on target. Of course, he's right. As usual. Despite T's current, ahem, distraction, if something happened to Jackie on my watch he'd be more irate than a dragon with a bee under its scales. Which means I need to return to the current Club Monster problem and be happy T decided against stalking Jackie, instead of stressing over his extracurricular activities.

Back to Jackie.

"Can we find the camera feed? See if she's on

there?"

Blue eyes widen as Smythe nods. "Great idea. Lucky for us, we're right by the offices. Come on."

He waves a hand at the camera hanging in the corner of the hall, presumably to scrub us off the recording. We try each door until we find the security office.

"Hey!" The only guard in the room rises from his chair, only to lose facial expression, his gaze blanking as Smythe mutters a spell. He sits, staring at the wall.

Nifty trick.

"You gonna teach me how to do that some day?"

Smythe raises a brow, silent speak for not fucking likely. I shrug.

"Help me look." He bends over the desk, typing commands.

Various camera angles flash on the screen, the tape rolling backward at a blurry speed until Jackie appears at the door of the restroom. She straightens her too-tight skirt, tosses her hair over her shoulder, a smile curving her lips. She heads in the direction of Donny's private room, but walks out of the camera view.

Smythe pushes more keys, causing another angle to appear. Jackie isn't as clear in this one as she walks through the crowd. Again, she disappears from view. Again, Smythe works his keyboard magic. This time when she appears, she's talking to the guy with the bad dye job.

A chill snakes down my spine as she laughs at something the man says. She gestures toward Donny's room, grabs the guy's arm, and leads him to where she thinks Donny awaits.

They disappear from view.

"Get her back! That's him! That's the guy who tried to kidnap me."

"Have patience." Several keystrokes later and the view in front of the private suite appears.

But not Jackie and the creeper.

"You missed them."

"No. See, the timestamp matches." He points to the time on the frozen image of Jackie taking the man's arm, comparing it to the time on the private suite.

"So where are they?"

Smythe pans several cameras. I see myself walking to the restroom after talking to Donny, who vanishes from all camera angles.

"Have you tried to access his private room?"

"Yep. There aren't cameras in there."

"Do you think that's where Jackie is?"

"There's only one way to find out."

Smythe strides to the door, holding it open for me as he waves a hand in the guard's direction. The guard blinks a couple of times, clearly coming out of his trance, as the door shuts behind us. When we arrive at the door into the club, Smythe mutters at the camera.

"Setting things to right?"

"Always. Come on. Let's see if she's in the private suite."

We hurry through the crowd, me wobbling in my heels after Smythe's long strides, arriving at the suite without generating many strange looks or alerting Donny's bodyguard. I yank open the door, poking my head inside.

The same group of players and their arm candies from earlier stare at me. No Donny to be seen.

"Where's Donny?"

"He left." One of the players answers.

"As in left, left. Or left to dance?"

"Does it matter? He left."

Shit. No help here. "Thanks."

I close the door, my heart pounding an uneven rhythm. Donny couldn't be responsible for Jenny's death, right? Or my drugged drink. It was a coincidence the bad dye job guy bumped into both me and Jackie shortly after we had been alone with Donny. Right? Someone that charitable couldn't be a murderer.

Right?

Geez, Gin, pull your head out of your ass. Of course charitable people could be murderers. Just because I didn't want Donny, the top giver to the local children's charity, to be a murderer, didn't mean he wasn't.

"I knew it." Smythe nods once. "There's something shady about Donny Football."

"Don't be ridiculous. It's a coincidence." I refuse to voice my doubts. Smother the suckers until they vanish. "Where do you think Jackie went? Is there a door between where she picked up that guy who tried to abduct me and here?"

Smythe looks at me a beat too long, his lips pursing as his eyes narrow. He draws in a breath, expression relaxing, and peers beyond my shoulder. "Over there."

He heads "over there," and I totter after him, my wobbling ankles keeping me from matching his strides. A door hides in the shadows, obscured by a tall table. Smythe ignores the KEEP OUT sign, shoving the thing open as if he owns the place. I teeter through as fast as possible before someone notices.

The door leads to another concrete hall lined with

rooms. Loud machinery sounds echo, a clear indication we've located the maintenance area. A great place to commit a murder. With all the noise, no one in the club would notice.

I shiver.

Smythe glances at me, one brow raised in an are-you-ready expression. I nod. He strides down the hall, opening doors, while I follow. The only thing out of place is a couple of dead cockroaches.

Nothing shocking for Dallas.

The hall dead-ends in a room containing the HVAC system and unrecognizable pieces of machinery. No Jackie. No bad dye job guy. No way out.

I activate the minion sensors in my eyes.

No minion trails.

"No trails."

Smythe nods. "Come on. Back to the club."

A deep bass beat throbs in my chest as we step through the door into the main club. Smythe leans against the closed door, arms crossed.

"Any suggestions where to go next?"

I shake my head. Was she dead? Where did my kidnapper take her? Or did he?

Smythe's eyes widen, then narrow as he looks past my shoulder. I start to turn to see what surprised him, when someone runs fingers from my shoulder to my elbow.

"Hey, babe." Donny's fingers dance against my upper arm. "You looking for me?"

I swear Smythe growls. Like a dog marking his territory. A little zinger of pleasure zips south at the sound.

Erasing fantasies of Smythe, I smile at Donny.

"Yeah. I was. Wanted to know if you've seen Jackie. We can't find her."

He nods. "She looked like shit, so I paid for a cab and told the cabbie to take her home."

Smythe straightens while I freeze. She could have been drugged. I'm pretty sure I looked like shit when Bad Dye Job guy tried to drag me out of the club.

"When?" Smythe recovers first.

Donny shrugs. "Just came back from putting her in the cab. Why's she so important? Because of your brother?" He raises a brow.

"Nah." I touch his arm. "I was giving her grief for dumping him earlier. She's important to the crime we're working on."

Smythe's glare bounces from my fingers on Donny's arm to my eyes, his jaw gritting. I drop my hand. The muscle in his jaw relaxes.

"Anyone leave at the same time you put her in the cab?" he asks.

"Sure. Do I know them? Nope. No one but her was in the cab, if that's what you're getting at. Care to tell me what Jackie has to do with Jenny?"

"Sorry. Active investigation." Smythe shrugs, as if apologizing for lying. "What's the address?"

Donny shrugs. "Some place off Spring Dale Road. Can't remember where."

Lucky for us he doesn't have to. The street is near my house in a string of low-income apartments. I'm assuming it's the same apartment T moved half his stuff into when they first started dating. Which was one of the few times I visited.

I know where it is. I've been there.

Smythe glances at me before giving Donny a single

nod. "Thanks. We appreciate your help. Let's go, Gin."

He reaches for my arm, but Donny beats him to me. Donny's arms wrap around my waist, and before I can recover from shock, he places a kiss on my mouth with the same lips he used on Jackie. A quick flash of their "dance" passes through my mind. Ugh.

"See ya 'round, babe." His fingers trail off my waist as he walks to his suite.

"What the fuck, Gin? He kissed you."

Smythe resembles a steaming pot, red-faced and boiling with jealousy.

I slip a hand on his chest, the strong *thump-thump* of his heart beating under the pads of my fingers. "Relax. He's just a friend."

"Do you always kiss your friends?"

"I didn't kiss him. He snuck one on me."

"You let him."

I raise a brow. "Yeah, because kicking him in the nuts would've been so much better. Geez, Smythe. What's your problem?"

"Him touching you, is my problem."

Okay. I'll admit it. His jealousy turns me on.

"Are we going to do this here or ensure Jackie is okay? Donny could be lying. Especially since my *justitia* thinks he's been around a demon or minion."

Smythe draws in a breath through his nose, holds it for a two-count and releases the air. "You said you know where her apartment is?"

"I've been there a couple of times."

"Then let's go."

He grabs my hand, laces his fingers with mine, the heat of his palm a comforting warmth. A frisson of jealousy mixed with possession wends through his thoughts before he snaps the connection closed on my empathic ability. This time his strides aren't as long, allowing me to walk beside him as if I'm his girlfriend, as if he's proving a point.

Which doesn't bother me like it should. I'm not normally into men who exude she's-mine, cavemen impersonations.

Despite strict adherence to trying to maintain a separation between my personal life and my professional life, my desire to continue on the high moral road appears to wane the longer I know Smythe. The more he touches me, the more he saves my ass from a variety of threats, the more I want to forget my eleventh commandment.

Circumstances sometimes dictate changing personal rules.

Cool, fall air greets us when we push through the door, the noise in the club subsiding to a pulsing bass deep within my chest. Smythe's jaw tenses, his fingers tightening. A fine tremor of ire passes from his palm into mine, an indication he has more to say about Donny's kiss once our hunt for Jackie ends.

Why does his jealousy turn me on? What is it about my mage guardian that makes me want to toss caution to the wind?

Why am I thinking about this now?

Stuffing Smythe fantasies into a corner of my mind for later review, I focus on the problem at hand: ensuring Jackie lives through the night.

Smythe remains quiet as he heads toward the alley lining the club. Once we're blocked from view of the street, he pulls out his phone, tapping the screen to bring up a map.

A couple of taps later and Jackie's apartment location pops into view.

"Would landing on this side of the building be best to remain unseen?" His voice shows none of the emotion vibrating through him. Only determination sounds in his tone.

I look to where he points. A satellite view of the apartment complex shows an overhead view of her building.

"I guess. It's dark. We should be good."

Smythe swipes the map clear, puts his phone in his pocket, then murmurs his portal-forming words. He grips my hand, leading me into the in-between and out by Jackie's apartment building. A chill releases me as we step into early fall air. Like I thought, no one stands around watching our appearance.

Smythe strides to the front of the building, me following at a slower pace. Heels should never be the choice of cat burglars. Or nurses who've stood on their feet all day.

My mentor is halfway up the stairs to Jackie's second-floor apartment before I even make it to the staircase. Maybe I should stay here.

When he arrives at the landing, he looks at me, one brow raised in a silent question. I point to my feet. He shakes his head. After a pause where he cracks a grin and gives a quick head shake at my refusal to move farther, he steps to Jackie's apartment, placing a hand against the door. His lips move as his eyes close. A yellow glow forms around his hand, sinks into the door, disappearing a second later.

After a moment the yellow light reforms around his hand, vanishing when he removes his palm from the door, his fingers balling into a fist. He meets me at the bottom of the stairs.

"No one's home."

"I could've told you that. No taxi can make it from Club Monster to here in the time it took us to portal."

"Your suspicion has been verified. We'll wait."

"Here? Where anyone can see us?"

"Don't be ridiculous." He raises a brow. "We'll wait where we landed. We can see the parking lot from there."

Once again I'm tromping through the grass in heels. Nice expensive heels not designed for lurking alongside buildings. Damn, my feet hurt.

But then again, that's what happens when you stand on your feet all day at work, then cram the suckers into pointy-toed shoes.

I lean against the building and pray no one calls the cops on us. Tiredness uses that moment to strike. I yawn.

"What time is it?" Pitching my voice to a low whisper, I elbow Smythe.

He pulls out his phone, turning it on and off. "A little after midnight."

"No wonder I'm tired."

"It won't be much longer."

As if his words summon taxis, one turns into the complex, headlights sweeping near where we hide. The taxi draws closer, stopping in front of Jackie's building. Did Donny tell the truth when he said he'd just put Jackie into a taxi? It seems like the drive would have taken longer, but then again, not much traffic is on the roads at a little after midnight on a Thursday morning.

After what seems like a minute of idling, the driver

opens the door, stomps around to the right back passenger side, and opens Jackie's door. He sighs loud enough for us to hear.

"Should've asked for more." If his words are meant to rouse Jackie, they fail.

The driver pulls her out of his cab, throwing an arm around her waist and one of her arms around his shoulders. She sags against him, her legs unable to support her weight.

"We should help." I start to move forward but Smythe grabs my arm, not allowing me to leave the shadows.

"Wait."

"What if the drug in her drink kills her?"

"It won't."

"How do you know?"

"Eloise said the drug in your system wasn't lethal. Jackie might be drunk."

"Seriously?"

"Shh."

I close my lips and press closer against the building. The driver escorts—more like carries—Jackie up the stairs. Since I can't see, I start to edge around the corner of the building, but Smythe stops me.

"He'll see us."

I nod, ears straining to hear what happens at the top of the stairs. Finally, I hear the sound of a door opening. Keys rattle as if pitched on the floor. The door clicks closed. Footsteps sound as the driver quicksteps down the stairs. He hops into his cab and drives off.

"Okay, let's go check on her."

"There's nothing to check. The drug will wear off. No one's in her apartment. We aren't watching her sleep." Smythe crosses his arms.

I stare at him. His eyes narrow as if daring me to oppose him. For a brief moment, I consider it. Jackie might be a ditz, but even ditzes deserve better than to be drugged and dumped in their apartment.

On the other hand, Smythe has a point. No one followed her here. I'm tired. And did I mention my aching feet?

"Okay. But shouldn't we make sure the door is locked?"

"Fine. I'll do it. Wait here."

Instead of waiting, I walk around to the front of the building. The best position for watching him check her lock. He places a hand against the door. The dull snick of the lock sounds a second before he removes his palm.

He joins me at the bottom of the stairs. His brow raise indicates he noticed my movement from his designated position. Whatever. He motions me back into the shadows where he forms a portal. The growl of an engine snaps my head around right when Smythe grabs my hand to step into the portal. Headlights flash near where we stand. Or maybe those lights belong to the kaleidoscope of colors lining the passage of the in-between.

The cold steals my breath, leaves chills on my skin as we land in my living room. Nothing but the tick of the kitchen wall clock greets my ears. No T. No Eloise.

"Why did you let him kiss you?"

Nothing, that is, except for a growling, jealous mage.

Chapter Twenty

Standing a few feet behind me, Smythe appears to vibrate, little green sparks popping around his head. His stance wide, his arms crossed, he looks like an avenging god. Instead of falling into my scared-of-the-big-bad-mage default mode, a wave of irritation crashes through me.

Seriously? He's accusing me of wanting Donny's kiss? Un-fucking-believable.

My fingers crank into fists as I balance on the balls of my feet. "I told you, he snuck one on me. You were right there. You saw it. What did you want me to do?"

"Well, shit. I don't know. Push him away? Slap him? Anything but stand there."

"Really, Smythe? He's a playah. Playahs kiss women instead of hugging them good-bye. He didn't mean anything by it."

"Are you shitting me?" His eyes flare as red tinges his cheeks. "You seriously think he didn't mean anything by it?"

Okay. So maybe he did. I shrug. "He doesn't matter to me. Just because I think he's innocent of Jenny's death doesn't mean I want to jump his bones. He's not the one I come home to at night."

"You mean T?"

"Geez, Smythe. You've got to be the densest man on the planet." I throw my arms into the air before turning on my heel and storming out of the kitchen.

I shove open the bedroom door, kick off my shoes, and am grabbed around the waist by a set of strong arms. A squeak escapes my lips.

"You really think I'm dense?" Smythe whispers in my ear, eliciting a set of chills that have nothing to do with the room temperature.

He shifts. The door clicks closed, sealing us in my bedroom.

"If the shoe fits."

"I'm wounded."

"Doesn't feel that way to me."

He kisses my neck, my ear. My knees threaten to loosen, remaining locked only because I'm not yet finished being mad at him.

"You really meant nothing by it?"

"Smythe. Donny's hot, but he's not you. I don't want him. I want you." So much for the Gin's eleventh commandment. When it came to Smythe, it was a stupid rule.

He twirls me around, hands at my waist, his gaze searching mine. "Do you?"

My stomach flutters as tingles spread through my limbs. I take a deep breath. Now or never.

"You mean something to me, something special. Donny's just a man with a football. You? You save my ass. Cook me dinner. Listen to me. It's you I want at the end of the day. Not him. You." I poke a finger at his chest. "You, Smythe."

He pulls me closer, crushing me to him as his lips devour mine. Lost in his kiss, his hands reverent upon my body, I barely notice when my dress falls to the floor. Or when the back of my knees hit the bed. He opens himself to me, his mind and soul weaving through mine until I no longer know where I end and he begins. His thoughts focus on me, on pleasuring me, us, his spirit a calming balm to my rocky soul.

My spirit relaxes, soothed into a tenuous peace. But unlike every other peaceful experience in my life, I'm going to make this last.

****

Bright noon light forces my eyes open. Smythe's arm lays heavy across my waist, pulling me against his warm, naked body. His breathing sounds deep and even, the gentle breath of the sleeping. Red numbers on the clock proclaim it to be 12:07 p.m.

After noon. It's been since my college days that I've slept this late. Of course, it's been since my college days I've stayed up most of the night making love.

I slip out from under Smythe's arm. He grunts, rolls over, and continues to sleep.

I've slept long enough. Time to get moving. A shower and clean clothes later, and I wander into the kitchen. The coffeemaker has long since turned itself off, the coffee cold in the pot.

"Hey, sleepyhead."

At T's voice, I start and release a high-pitched squeak, my hand clutched against my chest. As if that will help my heart stop pounding an off-beat drum-line. My twin leans against the frame between the living room and kitchen, a curious expression plastered on his grinning face.

"God, T, you gave me a heart attack." He reaches for me, and I step into his quick embrace, giving him a whack on the shoulder for good measure. "What are you doing here? Shouldn't you be at work?"

"I called in. Better things to do."

"Like what?" I glance behind him, half expecting to see Eloise in the living room. She's not.

"Making sure you're okay."

"Right as rain." I pour coffee into a mug and place the thing into the microwave. No sense wasting good coffee. I tilt an empty mug to T, while raising a brow. He shakes his head. "Why wouldn't I be?"

"He's in your bed." He tilts his head toward my bedroom. As if there's any doubt to whom the "he" refers.

I manage not to roll my eyes at his overprotective brother stance. Go me. I counter by pointing out the obvious.

"You had Eloise over last night."

"She wasn't in my bed when I woke."

"Ah-ha! So you admit something went on."

Red splashes his face. But only for a moment. "This isn't about me. It's about you. And him. He'll hurt you worse than Blake."

The microwave chooses that moment to ding, giving me the chance to master my surprise under the guise of pulling out my mug. Hurt me worse than Blake?

"What do you mean by that? Blake's dead." A fact I still grieve. Much less than I used to, though. More than my lover, Blake was my friend. I'm not sure you ever recover from losing a friend.

Especially when that friend was killed by a vengeful demon.

"When he leaves—"

"You're assuming he will."

"You actually think he plans to stay around? He's

using you."

"You say that about every man who shares my bed." Not that there have been a lot lately. My little touch-and-see ability makes sex with most men an odd experience.

"Not everyone." He gives me a pointed look.

I roll my eyes. "Okay, I get what your problem was with Blake. I was usually the other woman in that relationship. I get it. But Smythe? There is no other woman. It's just me. And I like the way he makes me feel."

"So he's good in bed. So are others."

"That's not what I mean." I pat my chest. "In here. He accepts me for who I am. My empathic abilities don't both him. It's freeing."

"Reading bodice rippers again?"

I give him a get-real look. "If you aren't going to listen, I'm not going to talk."

He throws his hands up in a placate-the-woman gesture. "Okay, okay. I've said my piece."

"He's different, I'm telling you."

Now it's his turn for the get-real look. Whatever.

"You gonna tell me why Eloise was over here last night?"

Red splashes his cheeks as he yanks open the nearest cabinet and pulls out a glass. Cha-ching. This is going to be good.

"She wanted to practice teaching me a spell to detect poison." He fills the glass with water, holds it toward me as if exhibiting an example. "Like what happened to you."

"Why bother with you? Shouldn't she teach that to me?"

He shrugs, takes a swallow. "Maybe she wanted to see me."

At least he's moving on. Even if the idea of him and Eloise belongs in the category of things that make me go huh.

"Maybe she did. Does that mean you're not feeling guilty about Eloise since Jackie is gone?"

Another sprinkling of red dots his cheeks. I circle my hand, encouraging his explanation.

"I was mad Jackie left. Hurt. You know. We've been together a year. It hurt that she wanted to leave."

"I'm sorry. That was a shitty thing for her to do."

"Yeah. So I thought, I'll get her back. I'll follow her around. She'll see that I'm better. But then I realized, while driving last night, I don't want her back. It wasn't the anger talking either. I realized what I liked most about her was how she made me feel in bed. That's not a good reason to stay in a relationship."

I blink once, then again for good measure. Yep. Still my twin. Stranger things really do happen.

"Gee, T. I never thought I'd hear you say that. Getting philosophical on me, eh?"

"I guess." One side of his mouth kicks up. "Took me awhile to realize it. Seeing Eloise helped. She's smart. I can talk to her about a lot. She says if I use my ghost-talker abilities they won't bother me as much."

I roll my fingers against my held mug, pausing to rehearse my reply. Forget it. I haven't had enough caffeine to rehearse much of anything.

"While I agree you shouldn't hide from your fears and face your abilities, she does know you used to talk to them all the time, right? And they still bugged you?"

His eyes narrow. Before he can say anything, the

rush of water flowing through old pipes squeals a dull background noise, an indication Smythe is in the shower.

I take a swallow of coffee, chasing it down with another.

T stops looking at my bedroom door as if it's going to explode, returning his gaze to mine. "She knows some of it. Not all."

No, not all. No one knows all. Only the two of us. Better that way. Safer. The fewer people who know how we disposed of our father, the smaller chance we have of getting caught.

"What are you going to do?"

He shrugs. "Not sure yet. Why did you contact me last night?"

So much for the Eloise thread. I've game-changed a conversation enough times to know when one's been thrown my way.

"We're tracking Jenny's killer. And the man who tried to kidnap me. We think they're related."

"I don't like it."

"I know. You've said that enough times. I'm fine."

"You weren't the other night. You could've been killed."

"I wasn't." I swallow another sip, trying to forget that night, forget losing control, forget how the drug cast my mind in darkness. My hands shake. I clutch my mug tighter. "Anyway, we went to Club Monster. Jackie was there."

T's face turns an interesting shade of mottled red complete with ticking jaw muscle. He knows she was with Donny despite me not telling him. So much for him being over Jackie. He sets his glass of water on the counter. When he speaks, his voice slides low and steady. If he wasn't my brother, I'd run the opposite way.

"She. Was. With. Donny?"

A rattling shakes the refrigerator, spreads across the floor, a spill of anger. I grab his clenched hand, pour calming energy under his skin.

"Maybe I should tell this story some other time. Not sure the fridge can handle it."

T draws in a deep breath. Holds and releases. The fridge returns to its normal operating background hum.

"I'm fine." He grabs my hand. "Go on."

All right then. "We lost track of her, despite finding the cameras. We saw her with the same guy who tried to kidnap me. We searched the club but didn't see either of them. Then Donny came up. Said Jackie looked drunk, so he hired her a cab. Gave us her address. We went to her apartment. No one was there. The cab drove up. Jackie was too drunk or drugged, so the cabbie carried her up the stairs. We made sure the door was locked, then we came back home. I contacted you because I wanted to know if you'd seen her. I thought you might have been at the club or lurking outside."

"She's safe?"

"She was when we left."

"What happened with her and Donny?"

Yeah. Not going there. Buying a new fridge is not in my budget. Lucky for me the doorbell uses that moment to ring. I glance out the kitchen window, which overlooks the street. A black and white police cruiser as well as an unmarked brown sedan are parked at the curb.

Not good. I'd rather be faced with the broken fridge.

T's eyes flare as the doorbell rings again. Keeping a hold on my coffee mug, I walk into the living room and open the door. Three cops stand on my porch, two obviously detectives, and one a blue-suited patrolman.

"Gin Crawford?" The black-haired detective asks.

"That's me."

"I'm Detective Jackson, and this is Detective Tinkle."

Tinkle? I press my tongue against the roof of my mouth to keep from grinning. I bet the poor detective was teased mercilessly as a kid with a name like Tinkle. Good thing neither detective seems to excel in mind reading. I nod to each detective.

"We're looking for your brother, Tonic Crawford. Is he here?"

T steps to my side, into their view, answering for me. "That's me. How can I help you?"

"May we come in?"

I step back, opening the door wide. What did T do to cause cops to show up at the house? Last I heard, they couldn't get you for thinking about stalking your ex, only if you carried it through. Which he didn't.

So why are they here?

"Mr. Crawford, where were you between the hours of one and three this morning?"

"Asleep. Why?"

"Anyone to confirm that?"

"No one was in my bed, if that's what you mean."

Detective Jackson gives T a pointed look. No humor in this guy.

"My friend and I came home around one last night.

T was here. I checked to make sure he was home." Which I didn't, but in this instance white lies about T never hurt.

"What about your friend? Did they see your brother?"

"I don't know."

"What's this about, Detective?" Smythe strides into the room like he owns the place.

Saved by the mentor. I flash him a thankful grin.

"We're trying to ascertain Mr. Crawford's whereabouts last night."

Smythe looks at T. My twin grimaces, then presses his fingers against his forehead.

"Sorry. Had a sharp pain," he mutters, his gaze striking Smythe in the eyes. *That son of a bitch just hopped into my mind.* His growl echoes in my head.

My mentor shrugs. "He was here asleep. As he said. May I ask what this is about?"

All three cops' eyes glaze as he compels them to speak. Nifty trick. One of these days he needs to teach it to me.

"A woman was murdered last night. Her body was left near someone's car in a similar manner as a murder last Thursday night. Mr. Crawford was known to date her, so we wanted to speak to him."

My shocked gaze meets T's. Color leaches from his face as he sways.

"Jackie's dead?" T's voice cracks.

Detective Tinkle nods. "Killed sometime last night. Know anyone who wanted her dead?"

T shakes his head, eyes filling with tears.

"Since he was here during the time of her death, he clearly didn't commit the crime. Unless you have any other questions, you should leave." Smythe gestures to the door, compelling the cops to leave. They give him puzzled looks but do as he asks, heading toward their cars.

As soon as they're out the door, I rush to T, wrap my arms around my twin. Silent sobs wrack his body. But he pulls away, dashing a hand under his eyes.

"You said she was alive. You said she was okay."

"She was, T. She was—"

"You lied to me! To your brother. Your own twin. Just—just leave me alone." He sniffs as he storms out, the front door slamming closed on his grief.

I stand frozen, my stomach twists, my heart tearing a jagged line in my aching chest. My brother, my twin, my other half wants nothing to do with me.

Tears well in my eyes. The revved roar of an engine snaps my attention. T peels out of the driveway, hauls ass down the street in the opposite direction the cops went. I sniff. He's gone. He's mad. He left me. What if he never comes back?

Smythe wraps his arms around me from behind. "He'll be back once he realizes you had nothing to do with her death. He's angry. Let him release it."

"How can she be dead?" I turn in his embrace until I face him. "You locked her door with your magic mojo. What happened?"

The tips of his ears flush red. "It wasn't magically locked. I used magic to turn her locks. Like a key. If I'd locked it magically, she wouldn't have been able to open the door until I magically unlocked it. And before you ask, yes, she was alive when we left."

"I saw headlights as we portaled away. But that shouldn't have been a cause for concern. It's an apartment complex." I sniff. "I can't believe she's dead."

Smythe rubs his hands in little circles on my back, a move no doubt meant to comfort.

"Let's look at the police report."

Releasing me, he gives me a quick peck on the lips before settling on the couch, computer on his lap. I make my way toward him with all the excitement of a condemned prisoner on execution day.

How can he think of police reports when T is upset?

"Gin, sit down and look at this." Smythe reaches a hand to me.

When I pause, he looks up from the screen, his gaze seeming to see into my soul, his blue eyes searching my face as if I'm an open book. Which I'm not.

I hope.

I take his hand. He has the courtesy not to compel me. And yet, a sense of calm washes around me. He's right. Again. T will return once his anger burns off. My twin's anger isn't meant for me even though I'm the target.

Patience is a freaking virtue I'm lacking.

I sit. Sniff. The ache in my chest eases, but remains.

"You'll be okay. Worry not, padawan. Look at this."

Instead of looking to where he points at the screen, I look at him. At the line of his jaw. At the way he exudes confidence. Opening my senses to him, I lean against his arm, soaking in his calm confidence. I could fall for this man. Hard. Harder than I fell for Blake.

T was right. Aidan Smythe had the potential to be my downfall.

Chapter Twenty-One

"They found Jackie in the parking lot of the Armadillo's practice facility. She was in the same position Jenny was, rose and all." Smythe taps the screen, ensuring I see the details of how Jackie's body was found.

Rage snakes through me, shaking my limbs. Jackie didn't deserve to die. Hiding behind the door when the good Lord passed out brains was no reason to be targeted by a serial killer.

That bastard was going down. Vengeance is mine, thus sayeth the demon huntress.

"Let's go. I'm going to hunt down that damn minion and show him the pointy end of my *justitia*." I give my wrist a shake, rattling the silver links of my bracelet.

Smythe taps a couple of keys, bringing up an aerial view of the practice facility, obviously scoping out the place for a good portal entry. After a few seconds of staring at the screen, he nods. Landing point obtained.

He snaps closed his laptop. "Ready?"

Without waiting for my reply, he stands, one hand facing away from his body. Muttering his portal-forming words, he opens a passage to the practice facility using the in-between. A few chilly seconds later, we step into the shadow of the building, along a side hidden from where Jackie was found.

Smythe strides around the corner, his body language telling all he belongs at the scene. I scramble behind him, mimicking his posture. I will catch this minion before he strikes again.

Activating the minion sensors in my eyes, I glance around the parking lot. Fire-engine red minion trails circle an area of concrete, thick enough to turn the ground blood red.

Or maybe that really was blood.

I swallow.

Yellow crime-scene tape rings the minion trails, hung on orange and white construction barriers, the notification of death a screaming warning. No body remains, but CSI folks wander the periphery of the circle, taking notes and collecting evidence. Detectives and blue-uniformed cops hover in the background as if waiting for the perfect time to strike.

Smythe strides to the sergeant in charge, flipping his magic badge open and closed.

"Special Agent Smythe and my consultant, Ms. Crawford. What happened?"

The sergeant blinks as do the detectives. Spell accomplished.

One of the detectives recovers first. "Woman by the name of Jackie Henderson found deceased in a spot reserved for one Donald Merryweather. Multiple stab wounds but very few defensive wounds. The body was laid out like she belonged in a coffin, flat on her back and holding a rose."

"Sounds like the Jenny O'Connor case from last week."

"Yep." The detective nods. "Several similarities between the two."

"Do you think the killer is trying to frame Mr. Merryweather?"

I'm pretty certain Smythe is one of the few people to refer to Donny as Mr. Merryweather. A strange urge to chuckle nails me, but I cover it with a cough everyone ignores.

"Could be. Or he's shitting in his own playground, if you know what I mean. Witnesses link him to both women. We could have a killer who's trying to frame the star, or we could have a star killing women and trying to make it look like he's innocent and being framed. I haven't decided which way to bet."

Smythe nods, while making a noncommittal noise. But I know better: he thinks Donny is as guilty as homemade sin.

Even if the minion trails prove otherwise.

Donny might be a lot of things, but my money's on him being innocent. Which begs the question of who killed Jenny and Jackie? Who wants Donny to pay for the crime?

I foresee another session of Smythe and his laptop tonight.

My thoughts trail down the rabbit path of other things he and I can do tonight, only to be yanked back to the present by the gravity of the situation.

Jackie was dead. Sleeping with my mentor should not be anywhere on my mind.

Color me a bad person.

"Was she dressed?" Smythe's words snap my attention back to the moment and off the rabbit trail of fantasies.

"Yep. Dressed to kill, no pun intended. Meant dressed up. Like she was out on a date. Her panties were missing so the ME will run a rape kit." He shrugs.

I hate to tell him, but the missing panties were about par for ditzy Jackie. I would say she left them off on purpose, but knowing her, she might have forgotten to wear them.

Smythe offers another one of his short nods, before shaking the detective's hand. "Thank you for your time."

"Sure. Always happy to help catch a killer."

I follow Smythe back to the side of the building where we appeared. Without saying anything, he mutters his portal-forming words and pulls me through the passage in-between. We land in my living room. My quiet, no-one-else-around living room.

The lack of T's presence sits heavy in my heart. But as Smythe said, he'll be back.

Eventually.

I hope.

"Did you see those minion trails?" Smythe stalks around the couch as if he holds a grudge against the cushions. "Are you sure Donny's not a minion?"

"Yes, I did, and yes, I am."

"Damn it. He's guilty of something. I know it."

"You just don't like him. He's a playah, but he's not a killer. We've been over this."

"You're too swayed by his charm to see him for what he is."

"Jealous much, Aidan?"

At his name, he stops, turns to me with narrowed eyes. Suspicion and surprise flit across his face. I should call him by his first name more often. I like the way it feels on my tongue.

Hell, I like the way *he* feels on my tongue.

Heat splashes my cheeks as I wipe that thought from my mind. Or try to. A little hard to wipe any thoughts when said fantasy stalks toward me.

I refuse to take a step back. I'm not afraid. I'm hot as hell.

He stops before he runs into me, close enough where I have to crane my head to look him in the eye.

"Always." His arms band around my waist, his lips press against mine, branding me his.

He needn't worry. Whatever this is between us encases me in a fragile hope, strings of peace binding us together. I want him with a ferociousness rarely felt, a twining of our souls, to believe we'll never part.

****

Hours later, we lie on my bed, contemplating another round. Our limbs entwined, my head resting on his shoulder, his hand stroking my upper arm, I realize this is what I've craved my whole life. This odd feeling of a fragile peace. Not even the bond with T relaxes me this way. Like a drug. The ultimate high.

But with none of the unwanted side effects.

I'm almost asleep when Smythe's phone buzzes, an annoying disturbance. He stiffens for a second before removing his arm from around my shoulder, twisting to reach for his phone. The twist fails to obtain the phone, which continues to buzz a warning from its resting spot on the floor.

Smythe leans off the bed, grabs the phone, swipes the talk button, and slams the thing against his ear.

"What?"

I roll to my side as he swings his legs off the bed to sit.

"What about Gin?" A long pause. "Okay. I'll be

right there."

My peace bubble bursts like a balloon on a rosebush. "Who was that?"

"The Agency." He leans over, giving me a peck on the cheek. "That minion from the attack finally cracked. All the mages are being called in to discuss our next move."

"What about the *Justitians*? Shouldn't we be there too?"

"They said not yet. Game plan before attack force." Pulling on his clothes, he gives me a wink. "Don't leave. I'll be back."

"When?"

His brow furrows. "Don't know. As soon as I can."

"And you expect me to stay here naked and waiting for who knows how long?" I tack a smile on my face, my effort to keep the disappointment out of my voice an epic fail.

"I expect you not to get into trouble while I'm gone."

"Do I ever?"

He raises a brow, silent talk for, Do I really need to answer that question?

"Okay, okay. I'll stay out of trouble. Oh master."

"That's mentor." He grins. "I'll be back as soon as I can. Don't try to track Jackie's killer without me."

"Don't be long. I'm missing you already."

After a lingering kiss, he portals to the Agency. I sigh, flopping onto my back. Memories of us drift through my mind, starting with our afternoon pleasantries to when we first met. Right after I stabbed my first minion. In my house. T ran out of his room with a shotgun, firing a round into the already-dead evil, a totally confused Jackie following.

Jackie. Poor, ditzy Jackie.

A shot of adrenaline sits me upright. How can I lie in bed, daydreaming about Smythe fantasies when her killer remains free? I'm a *Justitian*. The murderer is a minion. A stab, a slash, and that bastard goes home to its maker via the Hell express.

How can I do as Smythe asks and sit here waiting for his return? Time is of the essence. What if the killer strikes again? God only knows Donny can't keep his junk in his pants with a club full of women.

What if another woman dies because I'm unwilling to go it alone? Nothing wrong with going it alone. I'm a *Justitian*. A kickass *Justitian*. I can take that minion down.

Despite Smythe's request.

Some things need to be done sooner rather than later.

Chapter Twenty-Two

An hour and a half later, I park outside Club Monster in an already crowded parking lot. Don't these people have something better to do than get drunk and/or laid at a club? Like a hobby? Laundry?

Geez Louise. The things I do to keep the world safe from minions.

I shut the car door, engage the lock, straighten my long-sleeved blue blouse and short black skirt, and stride to the already-forming line in my toe-pinching expensive shoes. Why did I not insist Smythe teach me his nifty compulsion trick? That would come in handy to bypass this line.

A breeze howls down the street causing me to cross my arms in an effort to stay warm. Top on the to-do list: learn the compulsion spell.

The pounding bass from inside the club pours out into the street every time the door opens. An echo beats inside my bones. I inch forward as the person at the front of the line gains entrance.

A big burly man steps around the bouncer, heading my way. Donny's bodyguard. I'm saved.

He points a finger at me. "Follow me."

Ignoring the jealous glares of the line-standers, I do as the man says. The bouncer steps out of our way, allowing us entrance into the bass-thumping club.

Hearing loss, here I come.

"How did you know I was in line?" I raise my voice to be heard over the music.

His shoulders roll. "Cameras."

Oh yeah. Donny must have cameras in his room that overlook the club entrance. Does he use them to determine which club-goer he wants to hit on for the evening?

Not that I care. At least not care on a personal level. But it makes me wonder how the mind of a man touched by a minion or demon works. Who does Donny know that is a minion? How close does one have to get to a minion in order for the demon essence to rub off?

Perhaps another lesson in Demonology 101 is in order.

The bodyguard opens the door to Donny's private room, stepping back to usher me inside. He closes the door behind me, reducing the sound level enough to hear speech without yelling. But he stays outside the room.

A quick glance around shows why. No one except for Donny is present. None of his friends. No wanna-be fuck-bunnies. No servers. Only Donny, who stands behind a table where a huge-ass bouquet of red roses sits. The sweet perfume of roses blankets the room. No wonder. Not only is there a bouquet of the flowers, red and white petals litter the floor like confetti at a New Year's Eve party.

What. The. Hell?

"What's up, Donny? Where is everyone?" I walk into the room, one slow step at a time, my gaze never leaving his face. My *justitia* shakes a warning. Donny's not a minion, but demon essence clings to the football star like dandruff.

He smiles, a knowing confirmation I performed exactly as he planned. So much for surprising him.

"You came back to me. I knew you would."

Good lord. Does he actually think I came here for him? Judging by the roses and petals, the answer would be yes. Through an application of willpower, I manage not to roll my eyes. "I came back to ask you some questions."

"Not more of being the investigator. You know you're here for me. Stop playing around." He picks up the bouquet and heads my way.

"Not playing." I point a finger at him. "You are the one link to two dead women. Why is that?"

He thrusts the bouquet toward me, giving me no choice but to grab it or let it drop onto my feet. Like most women, I'm a sucker for roses. Despite them implying acceptance of his advance.

"You don't believe I killed those two women. You wouldn't be here if you did."

Okay, so he's right on the first part of that speech. Not that I'll tell him.

"Donny. My job is an investigator." More like minion killer, but investigator sounds more appropriate in this situation. "You are under suspicion."

"Not by the police." He shakes his head. "They cleared me. I have an alibi."

"You're still a link between Jenny and Jackie. My partner—"

"You left him at home tonight. Which means I'm right." One side of his lips kicks up. "You want me. You know you can't resist Donny Football, babe." He rubs a hand along my arm, his eyes full of lust.

I thrust the bouquet against his chest. Now it's his

turn to grab it or drop the roses on his shoes. Anger flashes in the depths of his eyes, a cold ire that spreads into my bones even though he's not touching my flesh.

The man clearly has never been told no.

"You aren't who I want. I'm here to discuss the case. Nothing more."

"Bullshit."

"What's the matter, Donny? Can't take no for an answer?"

Oops. That might not have been the smartest thing to poke the proverbial bear. The flash of anger seen earlier in his gaze morphs into a full-fledged forest fire complete with exploding trees and a raging wall of burning underbrush.

I was wrong. So wrong. Donny is capable of killing a person.

He shoves the bouquet into my chest, gripping my arms when I grab the roses.

"I want you. He said this would ensure I had you."

"Who—" But the rest of my sentence dies on my lips as he yanks me into a crushing kiss, complete with tongue thrust.

His thoughts of taking me against the wall slam into my mind. Yuck. Trying to pull away fails to work. I shove at his shoulder with one hand, raising my foot to stomp in his instep.

Loud music from the club sounds as the door bounces against the wall.

"What the hell?"

At the sound of Smythe's voice, Donny releases me. Thank God. I'm saved.

I turn to my mage, my lover, but his eyes hold nothing except steely contempt. Surely he doesn't think

I wanted Donny to kiss me?

"Smythe?"

"When I got to your place and found you gone, I thought I'd find you here but was afraid you'd run into trouble." His eyes narrow. A tic twitches the muscle in his jaw. "I guess not." He starts to leave.

Shit.

"Smythe, wait!" I take a step toward him as he pauses, one hand on the door. "It's not what you think. I came here to question him."

"Looks like you chose a different way of extracting answers."

"He came on to me! I told you how I felt. Nothing has changed. You're the one for me."

"Stop." He raises a hand. "Just stop. You're an adult. If you want Donny, you can have him." With those words, he steps into the club, slamming the door behind him.

Donny laughs as I stand frozen, staring at the last place Smythe stood, the air in my lungs balling into shards of ice. How can Smythe believe I want the laughing perv? Why did he not believe me? What can I say to stop him from leaving?

Say? More like demonstrate. I need to show him what he means to me. I am not letting Smythe walk out of this club. No way. He's mine.

Ignoring the expanding pressure in my chest, I pitch the roses on the nearest table and stride to the door. My hand reaches for the knob, but the door opens, almost hitting me in the face. A shaking of links against my wrist indicates my *justitia* turned into a sword. Holy shit.

Rahab, the demon I fought in the parking garage at

work, stands before me now, dressed in an expensive black suit. Not that his appearance matters in a fight. I will take him down. I'm better than him.

And yet I stand frozen as if under a demonic compulsion spell when he walks into the room. The same minion who attacked me in the hospital parking garage and the guy with the bad dye job follow him inside.

Triple shit.

Smythe! I shout using telepathy. *Come back! There's a demon!*

But he's blocking me. Or ignoring me. Damn it.

The door closes, locking me in with the trio from Hell and Donny.

Who dies first?

"I know you." Donny points at the minion. "You kept trying to talk to me last week. Like you knew me."

"That's because I do know you, asshole. Don't you remember me, Damian Spohn, from college?" Anger wraps the minion like a cloak of trembling rage.

"Damian?" The football star stares at the minion as if he saw a long-lost friend.

"Yeah…" Minion, aka Damian, points to Donny. "…you always one-upped me in college. Got all the girls. Guess what, asshole? I found me a way to take them back from you."

A flash of rage melts the ball of ice in my chest. Jackie was killed because some jackwagon was jealous of Donny's penis? At least he helped settle the issue of who I kill first.

Donny's jaw clenches. "I thought we were friends."

"That's what you get for thinking."

Rahab chuckles. "Boys, boys. Don't fight over the women. There are plenty to choose from. Like this lovely example." He points to me. Just what I wanted. To be singled out by a demon.

Wait a minute. Why am I standing around staring at said demon and its minion instead of blasting their asses back to Hell? Clearly, Smythe is not coming back. I'm on my own.

No problem. I've fought them once. I can fight them again. And win this time.

I drop my purse and step out of my shoes. Walking in the things was difficult enough. No way I could send this demon to Hell while wearing the pointy-toed heels.

"She doesn't want me." Donny shrugs. "Nothing I tried worked. Not much you can do about that, no matter what you say."

I lower my partially raised sword arm. What does he mean, "no matter what you say"? Has he spoken to Rahab before?

Well, duh, you idjit. Of course he has. Why else would he have demon essence clinging to his skin like a rash? He might have gotten that reaction from Damian, but his surprise at seeing his old "friend" rang true.

What does Rahab want with Donny? Maybe I should find out before annihilating his ass.

Or not.

The demon smiles, all chills and shivers. "I say join me. Or I'll give your lady love to him." He points to Damian, who eyes me like I'm a tasty peach.

Oh, hell no.

Donny glances at me. "And if I join? Do I get her?"

"Of course."

"Hey, hate to tell you, but I have some say so here." Do they actually think I'm on board with their crazy plan?

"So you think." Straight, white teeth flash in Rahab's mouth.

"So I know." Enough talking. Time for some slicing and dicing.

I draw back my sword arm at the same moment Donny answers the demon.

"I accept your offer."

Shit. So much for killing the minion first. If I want to save Donny from minion-hood, I need to wipe this demon off the face of the earth.

No problem.

Sword raised, I let loose a yell, taking a step toward the demon. Damian leaps in my way, pushing my arm to the side as he slams a fist into my jaw.

Ouch! My head snaps to the side, but the *justitia* overrules my nervous system, obliterating the pain. I use my body's momentum to continue into a twist and duck, bringing my sword up to stab at the minion's stomach.

My *justitia* slips through flesh like a knife through gelatin. The minion drops to the ground, clutching his stomach, blood leaking between his fingers. Wasting no time, I draw my arm back, my opposite hand grasping my sword wrist as the *justitia* slices through the minion's neck. Gray mist, the demon's essence, tries to return to its host, streaming out of Damian's neck and stomach.

But I catch it on the side of my blade, smiling as it hisses, as it dies. That part of the demon will never return to its host. Kill enough minions with a *justitia*, and the demon will die.

I glance at the stiffened demon. Yep, hurt him a bit. Score one for the demon huntress. So not sorry to kill his sustenance-giving minion.

A blow to my head has me falling forward. Double ouch. Again, my *justitia* earns its keep by shutting down my pain receptors. Unfortunately, it can't do a damn thing for the room spinning a crazed dance.

Hearing a rush of air, I roll, bringing up my sword. Bad Dye Job stands over me, shaking his fist. Ignoring the black dots dancing in my periphery, I stand, backhanding him. He drops, and I kick him in the side. Hard. Bastard.

But despite his accomplice-to-murder status, because he's human I can't kill him.

After another kick ensures me he's going nowhere, I turn my attention to Donny and the demon. Rahab's essence floats in the air between them, slowly going toward a wide-eyed Donny. The man's attention isn't on the demon or the essence about to give him minion status, but instead his full attention rests on me and the bodies scattered amongst the rose petals.

He might be an ass, but he doesn't deserve to become a minion. Not if I can help it. Which, lucky for him, I can.

Circling to the side, I rush the pair, aiming for the demon essence. If I can slice my *justitia* through it, then I can stop the transfer of evil to Donny.

But the demon catches on to my plan, moving to block me. As I swing my sword at him, he ducks, slamming a fist into my stomach. I double over, bringing my arms down to stop his upward kick.

"What is she?" Donny asks.

"A fucking *Justitian*." Rahab growls, stepping back as if to regroup.

"A what?"

The demon ignores the question, preferring to aim a punch at my jaw. I avoid him, twisting around, using my ears to locate where the demon stands. As soon as I complete the turn, I stab the *justitia* where the demon stands, only to come to a wide-eyed, frozen stance stop.

It's not the demon I stabbed. It's Donny.

Who is still a human.

Oh fucking shit.

Chapter Twenty-Three

Air gurgles in the back of Donny's throat, his hands wrap around the *justitia* with a weak effort to remove the sword from his chest. Blood gushes around the wound. I can't breathe, can't talk, can't disengage my sword. I stare at Donny, my wide-eyed expression mirroring his. We drop to our knees at the same time. His lips move. His eyes close. He topples to the side.

I don't need a nursing degree to tell me he's dead.

I killed him.

Oh God. What do I do?

"You fucking bitch!" Rahab steps into my line of view, hands cranked into fists. "You killed my best chance at power. Both of them!"

The demon wavers, as if shaking with rage. Or tears blur my vision. I swipe a hand under my eyes as I free Donny from my *justitia* and stand. I'd rather face demon wrath on my feet than cowering on the ground.

"Sorry?"

He growls, low and rumbling, a warning of an impending avalanche of death. "You killed two of my best minions."

Fact check, demon. I only killed one.

"Donny wasn't a minion."

"He would've been if you hadn't killed him, you worthless piece of shit. Prepare to die."

Borrow movie lines much, demon? Maybe he

learned conversation bits at Cheesy-Lines-R-Us.

I barely have time to fall into a fighting stance. His fist flies from the right, smacking me on the shoulder when I move to avoid being hit. I swing my *justitia*, but he jumps out of the way. Side-stepping to avoid Donny's body, I drop my guard, receiving a bruising blow to the ribs for my inattention.

I drop. Roll. Pull my feet under me. But he's on top of me quicker than an alligator on fresh meat. My head jerks to the side when his fist smashes into my jaw. Damn that hurt. Rahab might throw cheesy lines, but he knows how to punch.

Lucky for me, my *justitia* continues to block the pain, allowing me to remain upright, if a bit off balance. I strike his arm, a dark line forming along the slice. He draws in a breath through his nose, one hand slapping over the cut.

"Bitch. That hurt."

I smile. "Really?"

"Where's your guardian? Shouldn't he be here?"

My smile falters, wanes.

"Oh wait—" Rahab's lips curl in a spine-shaking smile. "He thought you cheated on him and stormed off. How quaint."

"How did you know that?"

"I have my ways."

"Fine. Don't share."

I try to draw on the power Zagan gave me, but nothing happens. Oh shit. By saving the Agency from the minion helicopter attack, I depleted my special-action red energy. No problem, though. I can do this on my own the old-fashioned way.

I rush Rahab, but he waves his hand, sending me

airborne sans one of Smythe's invisi-mats. My arms and legs windmill, as if hoping the movement will slow my momentum. Fat chance.

Right before I crash into the wall above the row of sofas, Rahab freezes me with another flick of his wrist.

"Tell your master, Rahab won."

Master? But before I can complete that thought, he flicks his wrist again, and my head slams into the wall with a sickening thud.

The room vanishes as my vision goes dark.

****

Softness cradles my body. My head throbs in time with my heart. Where am I? Why does my head hurt so badly?

And then memories assail me. T storming out, blaming me for Jackie's death. Smythe abandoning me, believing I betrayed him. Donny dying by my sword. Oh God, I killed a human. He might have been a step away from a minion, but he was still human when he died. Pain, like a ball of ice, pings around my chest, a loose bullet bent on destruction.

Memories of fighting Rahab cause my lids to snap open. Donny's private room lies in shambles, tables knocked over, bodies lying at odd angles. No demon.

The only good thing in this SNAFU.

I lie on a sofa, sword retracted into bracelet form, limbs crooked and aching. A quick body check complete with finger and toe wiggles proves nothing is broken, only bruised. I touch the back of my head, wincing as my fingers encounter a wet lump the approximate size of a small boulder. Damn demons.

No wonder *Justitians* have mage guardians. I would have won that fight if Smythe had been here.

Another mess to fix. What do I do without Smythe?

Get a grip, Gin. Call him.

My purse and shoes lie near the door, by the minion's helper. The room spins as I sit, walls moving when they should remain still. Music pounds, the bass rhythm amplifying the pounding in my skull. Vertical is not my friend. Instead of standing, I roll off the couch and crawl toward my purse.

My fingers touch the strap right as the door opens. Music floods the room. Donny's bodyguard stares at me, takes in the destruction, returns his wide-eyed gaze to me.

Oh, shit. I forgot all about him.

Don't see me, don't see me, don't see me.

He blinks, brows furrowing as he stares at me, through me. Cha-ching. The power of the *justitia*. Mention "don't see me" three times, and somehow I vanish from view. A skill I've used before to escape Smythe when we first met.

The bodyguard's gaze lands on Donny, and with a shout, he rushes to the downed football star, the door swinging shut when he releases his grip on the knob. I use the distraction to grab my purse and stuff my feet into my shoes. Slipping through the door takes only a moment despite being on my hands and knees. I no longer care if the bodyguard notices the door opening on its own.

The flashing lights blind me for a second, the strobes hurting my eyes, my head. Damn demon and his toss-the-*Justitian* power. Using the wall as a support, I manage to pull upright. The room swims, but only for a second, thanks to the healing power of the *justitia*. After a moment of using the wall as a prop, I hobble to the private restrooms, avoiding the clubbers. The third door opens, and I lock myself inside.

Once more I try to telepathically call Smythe, but again, he ignores me. Nothing left but to call him. I pull out my phone and scroll through my contacts until I find Smythe's number. A quick touch on his name and the call goes through. Only to be rerouted to voicemail. I try it again. Still voicemail on the second ring. Come on. Answer already. A third try gives the same result. Clearly he's ignoring me, sending me to voicemail instead of answering.

Well, fuck him. He once gave me the number of the Agency cleanup crew in case of an emergency. Him not picking up is an emergency. Especially since this club meets the definition of crime scene.

I find the cleanup crew number and place the call. A gruff voice answers on the second ring.

"Yes?"

"This is Gin Crawford. I need to request the cleanup crew be dispatched to Club Monster in Dallas."

"Where's your guardian?"

"Can't reach him."

"Any humans involved?"

"Yeah. One noticed, one's dead, and one's unconscious."

Gruff Voice curses. "We'll be right there. Don't move."

I push the end button. The wall cushions my backside as I sag against it, using it for support. My knees threaten to give out, but I stiffen them, refusing to allow my butt to touch the bathroom floor.

What seems like an hour passes before several kaleidoscopes of color appear, portals of the incoming cleanup crew. Four men and two women stride from the portals, glancing around the bathroom in confusion.

"We were told a cleanup is needed?" the tall brunette woman asks.

I straighten. "Yeah. Follow me."

We generate stares as we leave the restroom along with a couple of smiles and nods. Ignoring the gawks, I lead the crew to the private suite. A security team meets us at the door.

"You can't go in." Security's palm faces us.

A dark-skinned mage pushes past me. "Stumbling drunks are fools, huh?"

The security guard blinks. "Drunks?"

The mage peers behind the guard into the room. All the recessed lights shine on high, transforming the room from its normal sexy dimness to shadowed light. Despite the lights being on, not enough light bulbs exist to obliterate all the shadows. More security mingles with the freaked-out bodyguard. The minion's helper sits at the table, a bruise forming beneath his eye.

Rage spikes through me when he glances my direction. Rage followed by a dose of I-showed-you-up. I tamp down both emotions, focusing on the mage/security guard interaction.

"Drunks messing up your place are an annoyance, huh?"

"Yeah, man. Drunks are an annoyance." The glazed eyes and flat tone clue me in that the guard fell under the compulsion spell.

"An annoyance, but not a reason to keep us out."

"You're right." He steps to the side, waving us into the room.

"Remember, you saw nothing but annoying drunks.

Nothing different than any other night."

"Yeah, man. Nothing different."

"Go back to your normal post."

"'Night." The guard walks away to raised brows from his fellow security.

"Hey!" Another security runs forward, only to be stopped by Compulsion Spell Mage.

"Drunks are an annoyance."

This time, the remaining guards along with Donny's bodyguard, fall under the spell, nodding their heads to the tale of the annoying drunks. Security leaves, but the bodyguard remains.

The cleanup crew gives the dark-skinned mage a puzzled look as if he's slacking on the spell. I pitch my voice low.

"He's the bodyguard for Donny Merryweather. Donny is the dead human."

"The football star?" The mage's eyes flare.

"Yeah." I swallow while rubbing my chest.

"Why didn't you say so?"

I shrug.

He curses. The other mages look troubled. I doubt they're as troubled as I am by this whole mess. My good deed of stopping the demon from making a minion out of Donny while saving women from a serial killer turned into a hot mess of epic proportions. What kind of *Justitian* am I to kill a human?

I shove those thoughts to a far corner of my mind. At the moment, I need to use all my concentration.

"The minion's a serial killer. Been preying on women at the club. The asshole sitting at the table is his helper, not a minion."

"That's just wrong." Compulsion Spell Mage

shakes his head. "Hey, man." He strides toward the bodyguard. "What happened?"

What happened? Isn't he supposed to suggest, not ask?

"I heard a noise, came inside. They were all dead! Donny was dead! And this girl"—his eyes look at me— "that girl, that one!" He points a shaky finger. "She was here but disappeared! Now she's back. What's going on?"

"You had too much to drink."

"I don't drink on the job."

"Tonight you did."

"No, I didn't."

The mage's fingers flex. "Okay, you weren't drinking. You saw a pretty woman and got distracted."

The bodyguard nods, compulsion agreeing with his moral code. "Yeah. She was hot."

"When you came in, you saw that one," the mage points to the minion's sidekick, "getting into a fight with Donny. He'd already killed this one." He points to the dead minion. "Stabbed him. Nothing you could do."

"What!" the sidekick, aka Bad Dye Job, tries to stand, bumps into the table, and flops back on the sofa. "I did not."

The tall brunette female mage walks to him, places a hand on his shoulder, and pulls a long, thin knife out of a holder strapped to her thigh. BDJ's eyes widen as he tries to escape the sharp point.

"You killed him. Don't deny it."

BDJ's mouth slackens, his eyes glazing. "I like to watch him kill."

"Yeah, you do, you sick fuck. Pick up the knife."

He does as told, twisting the blade back and forth,

as if fascinated by the reflections of light on metal. The female mage keeps her gaze glued to the knife.

"See—" Compulsion Spell Mage points at BDJ. "—he killed Donny."

"Yeah, you're right." The bodyguard nods. "But why?"

The mage looks at me, making a rolling gesture with his hand. I clear my throat.

"The dead…guy"—I point to the minion—"stalked Donny. Was jealous of his fame, so he killed the women Donny slept with. He and the bastard over there"—I point to BDJ—"would drug the women, but tonight they confronted Donny. That guy"—another point to BDJ—"went crazy and stabbed the dead guy. Then he stabbed Donny."

The bodyguard nods, believing my story for the truth. Most of it was. And it caught the sick fuck who liked to watch the minion kill defenseless women. Why couldn't I have killed him instead of Donny?

I rub my head. No time for those thoughts. No time to ponder the what-ifs and whys. Or to glance at Donny's body, to see the blood congealing in a pool leaking from under him. I squeeze my eyes closed.

"Nothing you could have done, man. When the cops arrive, you can tell them what happened. This little fucker"—the mage points to BDJ—"killed Donny. And a bunch of women. And the dead guy, although he did everyone a favor there. You understand?"

The bodyguard nods. "Awful night."

"That it is, my man, that it is. Now sit next to that crazyass fucker with the knife and forget what you're about to see."

With a shrug, the bodyguard sits next to the

minion's helper, both men staring unseeing as the cleanup crew starts working.

"What do I need to do?" I ask the Compulsion Spell Mage.

"Nothing. You've already done enough." He points to the door. "Leave."

Good idea. I want to get the hell away from this club.

"Thanks for helping."

His piercing stare stabs me. "That's our job. Now leave."

Sound fuzzes by, voices calling, an annoying background noise. My hand touches the handle of my car door, its lack of opening motion snapping me into the present.

I stand in the crowded parking lot by my car, purse clutched in one hand, keys in the other. My head throbs, despite the *justitia's* healing influence. How did I get here?

Oh, right. Compulsion spell. Not only am I clearly not consistent with thwarting it, but Smythe needs to teach me that nifty trick.

Provided he talks to me again. Damn man. Wouldn't even let me explain. And refuses to answer my calls. Maybe he'll respond to a text.

Pushing the key fob, I unlock the door, slide into my seat, and engage the locks. I send a quick text to Smythe.

It's not what you think. Call me. Something happened.

I put the phone in the cup holder, so I can hear it ping when he returns a response. Which he doesn't do in the thirty-five minutes it takes me to get home.

My house sits dark, abandoned. No cars are out front, which means T found someplace else to bunk tonight.

T? I try calling him telepathically, but like Smythe, he refuses to respond. My shoulders quiver, my stomach turns into a ball of stones. I open the garage door, pulling into my spot, tears trailing down my cheeks.

I killed Donny. I killed a human, a human who did not deserve to die. Perhaps Smythe and T's lack of response is punishment for my crime.

How do I atone for a crime when no one knows what I did? The cleanup crew doesn't count. How do I make things right?

I can't. I can never make things right. It's like when I was a child, nothing I did stopped the beatings. Nothing I did stopped my father from hurting us. Nothing I can do will help.

Dashing the tears off my face, I get out of the car, walk to the back door. I unlock the kitchen door, step inside, and throw the deadbolt. As soon as I flip on the lights, I freeze. Unlike my limbs, my *justitia* vibrates its happy-to-see-you dance, which only means one thing.

Or one demon.

Zagan stands in my kitchen, arms crossed, legs shoulder-width apart, an avenging demon out for blood. Light gleams off his olive skin, his muscular forearms accentuated by the rolled sleeves of his white button-down shirt. Black trousers complete with loafers round out his outfit as if he came from a date. The thought of which almost, but not quite, makes a grin tease my lips.

I wipe the expression from my face as soon as it appears, but not soon enough. His eyes narrow, his lips twitch as if he fights a snarl.

"You lost."

My eyes flare. How did he know? And why would he be this upset over it? Shouldn't he be happy I failed to kill a demon, one of his kin?

At least, I'm assuming they're kin. Yep. Definitely need to pull out the Demonology 101 textbook for another read-through.

"What? Nothing to say? I gave you the ability to win, and you wasted it."

Anger loosens my lips. "It wasn't a waste. I saved lives with your energy."

"Mage lives." He slices a hand through the air.

"What? Have a problem with mages?"

He takes a step closer. Of course he has problems with mages. They keep trying to kill him. Stupid, stupid, stupid to egg on a demon.

Even if he is a demon I like.

"You"—he points a finger at me, eradicating any doubt he refers to another—"fail to understand what is at stake."

"Enlighten me."

"Why? You. Failed. Me!"

I take a step back, run into the door. My *justitia* stops happy dancing on my wrist, but refuses to turn into a sword.

Not that I could kill Zagan even if it did.

"I didn't realize you'd be upset over me not killing a demon."

"I didn't realize you would waste my gift."

"It wasn't wasted."

"You wasted it on minions."

"Then why do you give me demonic power if not

to kill demonic entities?"

He takes a step back, eyes narrowing on me as if testing my intelligence and finding it lacking. "You would not understand."

"Try me."

"No. You wasted my gift."

"You're starting to sound like a broken record."

"A broken record?"

"You're repeating yourself."

He takes a step closer, then another, until he stands close enough I can feel his heat. I shrink against the door, trying to get as far away from his touch as possible. Empathic abilities plus demon touch equals brain hemorrhage. The last time he touched me, my *justitia* had to work overtime to block the tangles of evil demon thoughts from rupturing my brain. Thoughts too twisted for human comprehension.

And yet I crave his touch. Crave him like an addict does a bottle. I crave him like the addict I am.

I put my hands on his chest. His heart pounds beneath the pads of my fingers. He looks at my hands, raising his gaze to my eyes as he grips my wrists over my sleeves in a bone-crushing grasp, pulling my hands away from his body.

"You. Failed. Me. Worthless human. You are like the others, not unique as I hoped. Worthless. You do not deserve my gift. You do not deserve this bracelet."

Power leaches from his hand, coursing into my *justitia*. The bracelet quivers, the entity along my nerves flaring to life as it draws on my energy to stop Zagan's spell. The silver links shift, transforming into a sword.

Zagan drops my wrists, leaping back to avoid the

blade. Red stains his white shirt from a line slashed across his chest. His lip curls. My breath rushes in short pants as he rubs a hand across the shallow cut on his chest.

"You ruined my shirt."

"You tried to spell my *justitia* into something it didn't like."

"I am tired of dealing with you and your lack of obedience." He slashes a hand through the air. "I am done."

With those words, he forms a portal, disappearing into a kaleidoscope of colors.

I slump against the door, my heart pounding, my eyes stinging. My knees forget their job, and I butt plant on the floor. With a pop, the *justitia* returns to bracelet form, the entity along my nerves performing the virtual equivalent of an irate pacing human.

Placing a hand over the silver links, I will it to calm. Memories surge, its memories, ancient and cold. Warm rocks. Bright fires. Multi-hued demons plotting, scheming. Words escape me, the language rolling in syllables I could never hope to pronounce, yet I understand the gist. My *justitia* ensures I understand.

One demon wants control of Hell. One demon will do anything to conquer, even if it means waiting millennia for the perfect occurrence of events. And all the other demons will do anything to stop him.

Hot tears press against the back of my eyes. Zagan abandoning me should make me happy. Being free of him, knowing he no longer attempts to make me his servant, should bring me pleasure.

All I want to do is cry.

First T. Then Smythe. Now Zagan.

I'm not crying over the demon. I'm crying over my fuckups.

I dash a hand under my eyes. Crying never got me anywhere. I need to suck it up, pull on my big girl panties, forget about this awful evening.

Kicking off my heels, I stand. Tingling shoots through my limbs, a desire to make it all go away. Leaving my bedroom window cracked tonight won't work, won't soothe me. One thing will.

I swallow. Ten years ago I promised myself I'd never touch another drop of whiskey. I broke that promise a week ago in the club. Which was bad, but not the drink that counts. It wasn't the bottle I stashed in the pantry, on the top shelf behind a box of trash bags. That bottle represented me giving up my habit, not allowing a substance to rule my life.

Starting a new life, one without hard liquor.

But that bottle would soothe the pain gnawing a hole in my heart, spreading fire through my limbs.

On numb feet I walk to the pantry. Pull down the box of trash bags. Stand on my tiptoes, fingers grasping the bottle. In my palm, the glass feels smooth, a calling to imbibe.

Ignoring my inner voice informing me of bad decisions, I twist open the cap, take a large swallow. Heat burns my throat, swirls in my stomach. A second swallow spreads the heat to my cold limbs. Falling off the wagon never felt so good.

Two more swallows and I'm in T's room, rummaging through his nightstand until I find what I need. With shaky hands, I light the blunt, inhale a deep breath. Relief courses through my veins, chasing away the cold.

So much for my new life on the straight and narrow. I'm worthless. Zagan's right. I killed Donny.

Taking another hit, I let the smoke soothe my raw nerves.

The room spins. Why am I standing? I lean against the headboard, drawing my knees to my chest. The heat from the bottle coupled with the smoke eases the ache residing against my heart.

I look at the bottle, at the amber liquid swirling behind clear glass. I take another large swallow, then another and another before dropping the bottle on the nightstand. Sometimes the worst demons aren't the ones throwing punches or energy balls, they're the ones hidden inside, invisible to the world.

Tomorrow, I'll get my act together. Tomorrow, I'll find T and Aidan. Make them see reason. Nothing will ever be the same, but tomorrow dawns another day.

A word about the author...

Karilyn Bentley's love of reading stories and preference for sitting in front of a computer at home instead of in a cube drove her to pen her own works, blending fantasy and romance mixed with a touch of funny.

Her paranormal romance novella, *Werewolves in London*, placed in the Got Wolf contest and started her writing career as an author of sexy heroes and lush fantasy worlds.

Karilyn lives in Colorado with her own hunky hero, a crazy dog nicknamed The Kraken, a silly puppy, and a handful of colorful saltwater fish. Find out more about Karilyn at www.karilynbentley.com